STRANGE DEVELOPMENTS

A DEGREES OF MAGIC NOVELLA

J.M. LINKHART

Published in the United States of America by
Goblin Booth Productions, LLC

This first paperback edition published October 2025

Cover design by James Mitchell Lewis and Jessica Linkhart

Interior design by James Mitchell Lewis

Maps and icons © 2024 by Jessica Linkhart and James Mitchell Lewis

Manufactured in the United States of America by IngramSpark®

ISBN 979-8-9926873-1-6

Visit goblinboothproductions.com
to learn more about this publisher and their projects.

To The Lore Writing Club
and many more successful sprints

1925 UNITED STATES

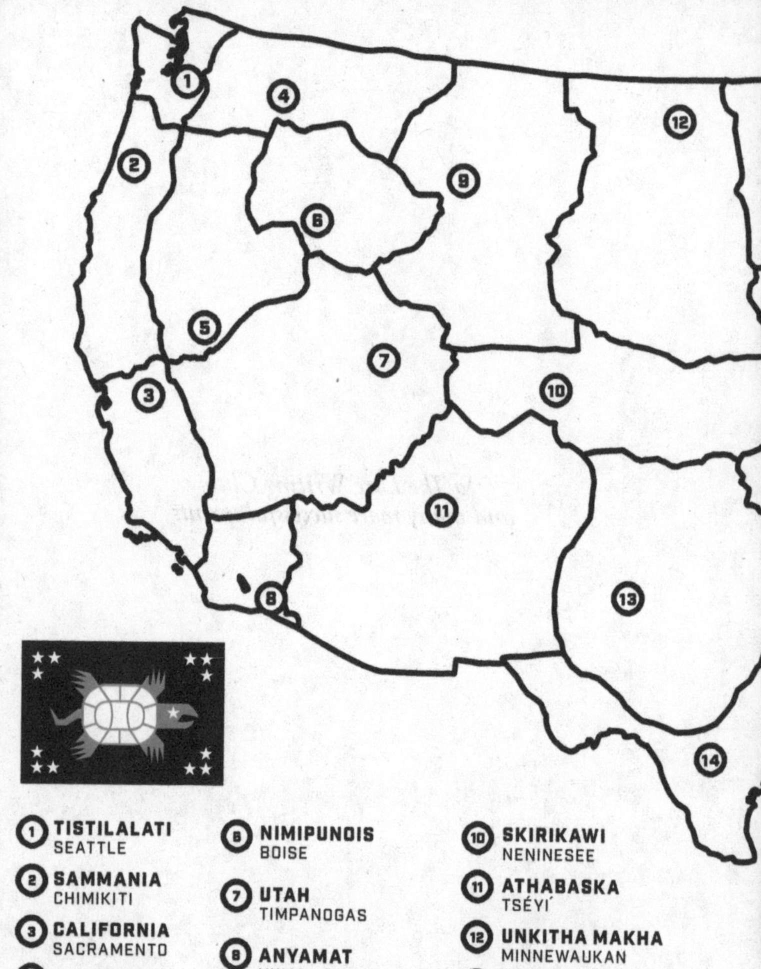

1 TISTILALATI
SEATTLE

2 SAMMANIA
CHIMIKITI

3 CALIFORNIA
SACRAMENTO

4 PATOKSKO
SPOKANE

5 WAGOPETIA
KOOYOOE

6 NIMIPUNOIS
BOISE

7 UTAH
TIMPANOGAS

8 ANYAMAT
YUMA

9 CHEYENNE COMMONWEALTH
EKHOVATOVA

10 SKIRIKAWI
NENINESEE

11 ATHABASKA
TSÉYI´

12 UNKITHA MAKHA
MINNEWAUKAN

13 COMANCHERIA
OHAKAHNIPI

14 TEXAS
SAN ANTONIO

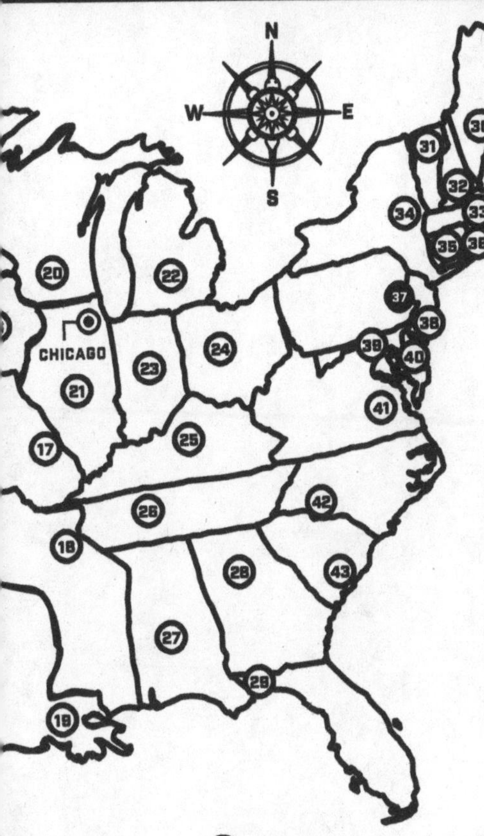
N
W
E
S
CHICAGO
25 KENTUCKY FRANKFORT
26 TENNESSEE NASHVILLE
27 JANATALLA AYN MAJID
28 WALLATIA ATLANTA
29 FLORIDA TALLAHASSEE
30 MAINE AUGUSTA
31 VERMONT MONTPELIER
32 NEW HAMPSHIRE CONCORD
33 MASSACHUSSETTS BOSTON
34 NEW YORK SCHENECTADY
35 CONNECTICUT HARTFORD
36 RHODE ISLAND PROVIDENCE
37 PENNSYLVANIA PHILADELPHIA
38 NEW JERSEY ATLANTIC CITY
39 DELAWARE DOVER
40 MARYLAND BALTIMORE
41 VIRGINIA WILLIAMSBURG
42 CAROLINA CHARLOTTE
43 ELENIA YOHANNESTON

15 MINNESOTA MINNEAPOLIS
16 IOWA DES MOINES
17 MISSOURI ST. LOUIS
18 MISSISSIPPI CHICKASAW BLUFFS
19 DJENNE LYON BATON ROUGE
20 WISCONSIN MADISON
21 ILLINOIS SPRINGFIELD
22 MICHIGAN LANSING
23 INDIANA INDIANAPOLIS
24 OHIO FRANKLINTON

CHAPTER ONE

BERNICE CHANDLER had not gone by the cemetery for two months, but she'd thought about it every day. And every day, there was a reason not to go. First it was raining and cold. Then muddy and slick. Then snowing. And there was work, always work. She was relieved by these distractions, these excuses—and she hated them for being so convenient.

Bernie was no stranger to death. But for all the experience she'd had losing people, she wished she were a better mourner. Or simply a better friend.

At first glance on that cold mid-October day, Bernie did not seem dressed for a pilgrimage to a graveside, though she had every intention of making one later. She was decked out in her full formal uniform: a crisp white dress shirt, a pressed charcoal walking skirt, dark stockings, carefully shined boots, and an immaculately pressed persimmon-colored overcoat sporting bright patches on either arm declaring her a Knight-Maiden of the Second Order. The one concession to her grief she wore that day was her black netella, wrapped around her shoulders and draped over her shorn, tightly-curling hair. Earrings of silver and pearl and a hint of makeup polished off her look. She'd have rather not bothered, but it was a necessity given the elegance of the event she was bound to attend: The Ladies Temperance League of Chicago's Annual Autumn Charity Luncheon.

While grateful for their help getting the vote, Bernie herself was not terribly interested in upholding the most obvious tenet of the Temperance Movement, being more than happy to bathe herself in bathtub gin whenever the occasion allowed. But she was not going for pleasure. She was working, and her work was of a peculiar stripe.

Bernie was a knight in The Order of Joan, the centuries-old organization tasked with protecting the mundane people of the world from magical threats—as well as magic-practitioners and other supernatural beings from the wrath of mundane ignorance. Her work, consequently, had quite a bit to do with magic, particularly where it intersected with the criminal, the monstrous, and occasionally—but not insignificantly—the violent. Hence the cruciform sword buckled at her waist, which was by no means a ceremonial piece.

Not that today's task threatened to demand its use. As Bernie sat quietly in her cab and watched the city slip by, she considered the case that had fallen in her lap rather suddenly that morning. It had arrived in a red folder, the Order's shorthand for an especially time-sensitive investigation. But a quick review of its contents left Bernie with more questions than answers, starting with why it was time-sensitive at all. It was a simple job:

someone was toting around an enchanted object they shouldn't possess and making a general pest of themselves, and her task was to confiscate it. From the information in the file, it seemed to be a Kodak Brownie number 2 camera, and whatever magical properties it had posed no bodily harm to anyone. Yet the file didn't go on to specify *what* properties, exactly, it held.

There was a simple explanation for that. The file had been light on paperwork and hastily assembled, suggesting that it had just come in—and more intriguing yet, it was a Coven Request.

While the Order worked with covens to keep the peace between magic practitioners and the oft-too-zealous religious masses, covens still strove their utmost to keep the Order out of their own business. That one of the Chicago covens had asked for the Order to intervene was highly unusual. The only reason given by the requesting coven was that the object was "a nuisance best kept from general circulation that ought to be relegated to some dusty Order cupboard for-ever more."

Whoever had taken down the information had apparently not held the request in high esteem. The mission would have been given to a Knight-Maiden of the First Order if they had, if not a Knight-Matron. Instead, it had landed on Bernie's desk; Bernie, who was but a lowly Knight-Maiden of the Second Order, and that for only a year. But then the Chicago Order was perpetually understaffed and overstretched, and it was October to boot—always a busy month for them. At first Bernie thought the red folder was given to her because some higher-up saw promise in her and wanted to throw her a bone. After reading through the file, though, she suspected the reasons were more political. This case honestly seemed like a waste of time, but a coven had requested it and emphasized a timely closure, which made it difficult to decline. Thus a compromise was struck, one that Bernie had become a part of: the case was expedited, but given to a lower knight who could better afford putting her other duties on hold for this nonsense.

Bernie would have liked it if the case had been given to her as a vote of confidence, surely, but she supposed this was acceptable, too. It was a sweet deal, getting to spend a day in the Crystal Ballroom of The Blackstone, rubbing elbows with the rich and the famous and nibbling on hors d'oeuvres as she kept an eye peeled for a magic camera. Capital luck, really. And even better, it would be a marvelous distraction from… Well, everything else.

Before reaching The Blackstone, she drew out a slender tube stoppered with an eyedropper from her pocket. A single drop of Optical Oil in her right eye brought a well of tears to both. When the pain subsided, the world looked slightly different, at least as seen from the right.

The cab interior smelled of layers of smoke, sweat, perfume, and spices, but now Bernie could see ghostly whispers of strong emotions yet to dissipate hovering in the close air: twin rosy twists of giddy joy, a curl of scarlet jealousy, a sickly spiral of worry, and the tell-tale blue-black blur of despair. And the cabby's flat cap had a glowing point inside it, some magic charm sewn into the lining. She wondered if he knew it was there, or if some wife or mother had added it without his knowing. It didn't have any unpleasantness about it that a curse or hex might, so she let it lie.

As they pulled up to The Blackstone, Bernie discreetly checked her make-up in her compact mirror and closed it, satisfied the tears prompted by the Optical Oil hadn't smudged her mascara. Then she stepped out onto the curb, shoulders squared and chin up, determined to make the most of this job with its promise of a lovely lunch and an easy win before sundown.

The first hour at the Temperance League's Autumn Luncheon was uneventful, almost painfully dull. Bernie had arrived early to better scope out the incoming crowd and make note of the photographers present. There were many, but that wasn't surprising considering the caliber of guests attending. DuSables, Loons, Mishimakwas, Polks, Wrigleys, and Okafors, to name only a few—the crème de la crème of Chicago society, though seldom were the heads of those estimable clans in attendance. More typically it was their wives or daughters; sons or cousins might also have been pressed to make an appearance in their absence. Bernie was mostly left alone to people-watch. Occasionally she was approached by nosey socialites, but her netella, worn in mourning fashion, seemed to keep most conversationalists away. She remained mostly the subject of curious glances, nothing more, which was just as well for her and her mission.

There was certainly plenty of magic to see. Trouble was, none of it seemed out of place. Like the cabby's charm, most of the magic centered around trinkets toted on watch chains or hidden in purses or jewelry. Protective pendants like the crystal bracelet around Bernie's wrist meant to deflect malefic magics, or baubles to subtly enhance the wearer's beauty in the eyes of the beholder. She spotted the aura of a spell for silvering the tongue, obvious to her by the glowing clouds issuing from a man's mouth like smoke from a dragon, but absolutely invisible to anyone else.

Yet every camera she laid eyes on was nothing more than what it seemed, from portable Brownies to modern Leicas to older, unwieldy box cameras on tripods. Not a shimmer of magic to any one of them.

As the hour neared one, she started seeing glimpses of coven witches in the growing crowd. They were easy for her to pick out: sparks of residual magic clung to their skin, their hair, their clothing, and danced like fireflies in their wake. Ten years ago, their presence would have been unusual, if not downright alarming at a place like this. Now, in the thoroughly modern year of 1925, it was almost expected. No longer confined to obscure private dealings with the lowly and powerful alike, covens were busily building public ties to respectable institutions all over the nation, determined to capitalize on the post-war fascination with all things magical. This was exactly the kind of event they would be keen to attend. Bernie noted an uneasiness shared between them, furtive looks that sometimes strayed toward outright hostility. But coven politics were messy, often strained, and there was no reason to believe there was anything more behind those looks than the typical ongoing rivalries. Bernie was savvy enough to know not to go putting her foot in the middle of things by asking any of them for the dish.

As the last quarter hour dragged on, Bernie idly wondered

what luncheon would be. She expected the mains would be the standard high brow fare: jolly rice, beef wellington, or ham. Wat or stew and swallows would be too plebeian for these rich cats, but kitfo might make an appearance. And boy, could she go for some kitfo right about now.

A vague headache she first attributed to hunger began to pulse behind her right eye as the effects of the Optical Oil slowly faded. Bernie cringed as a spike of pain shot to the back of her head.

"Excuse me, miss, might I take a photograph of you?"

Bernie lowered her hand from her temple and blinked. A young man stood before her, a junior of hers by only a few years, perhaps somewhere between sixteen and eighteen. He had warm brown skin a few shades lighter than hers and wide, dark eyes. His suit was pressed but a little tight, like he had grown since it had last been tailored.

He smiled in what he obviously thought was a charming way, and it was charming, but not for the reasons he believed. He meant it to be flirtatious, but it just emphasized his youthful inexperience to Bernie. It was sweet.

"Might as well," she said, returning his smile wryly. Several other photographers had already snapped hers, why not another? "What's the point of coming to one of these things all dolled up if no one takes notice?"

The boy laughed, positioned the camera just so, and pressed the shutter lever.

Bernie flinched as a swarm of pinpricks burst across her right eye. The infamous Optical Oil headache was worsening—

and it'd be even more unbearable later, since she would have to use another drop soon. The hint of magic from the attraction amulet hidden in the silverwork of the nearby debutante's broach seemed to have faded entirely.

The boy thanked her and she nodded vaguely, scanning the venue for the ladies room to touch up on Optical Oil.

"Excuse me, miss, I don't mean to be forward, but… if I may ask, who did you lose?"

Bernie turned back to him, surprised.

"Pardon?"

He dipped his head, his cheeks coloring slightly. "I recently lost someone myself. I—well, my apologies. I shouldn't have asked."

Bernie studied him for a moment. Yes, she could see it now, a familiar kind of tarnish just beneath the shine of his smile and his formal duds.

"Her name was Dot—Dorothy," she said softly. "She was my friend."

The boy nodded and swallowed hard. "May the Almighty give you patience and ease to pass through these trials."

Tears suddenly pricked her eyes, a familiar (and damn inconvenient!) sensation over the last two months. Disarmed, she found she could only nod back.

After a brief, solemn silence, the boy looked up at her with a sheepish half-smile rendered entirely disingenuous by the glint of mischief in his eye.

"Not a husband, then?"

As suddenly as the tears had come, they were dispelled with

a laugh. It made her eye throb, but she welcomed it anyway. It had been a long time since she'd laughed.

"No, not a husband, and I daresay you're too young to do the job." She flashed him an indulgent smile. "Now go on, shoo. I'm sure you have more important people to photograph, and your boss will have your head if you waste time flirting with a wallflower like me."

"You're no wallflower," he said in parting, and winked.

He was right. She wasn't.

"Only when I'm sober," Bernie murmured to herself as she made her way to the bathroom.

But she stopped short when she heard a familiar voice followed by a gale of laughter somewhere to her right. Almost as if by magic, the crowd parted when she turned her head, giving her a clear view of the speaker. She clenched her teeth so hard she was surprised they didn't crack. Because there he was, the son of a bitch, in all his fake oily charm and genuinely expensive finery. Dot's old flame. Still here, damn him, while she was gone forever, buried under six feet of dirt and stone.

As usual, he carried a perpetual cloud of cigarette smoke around him. It left the burning end of his fancy crimson-papered cigarette and wrapped itself lovingly around him in drifting loops and curls before floating further into the room or sinking into the wool of his smartly-tailored charcoal suit. His bleached-white hair shone under the ballroom's lights, though nowhere nearly as bright as his preternatural eyes, their irises a molten, glowing gold, would be if he hadn't hidden them beneath his signature black-tinted glasses. He laughed again at something a pretty young thing desperate to win his attention said, his perfectly white teeth flashing in the cruel curve of his mouth.

Valentino Morandi, Chicago's own devil, was somehow, incredibly, against all logic, *here* at the Temperance League's Autumn Luncheon.

CHAPTER TWO

✣✝✣

BERNIE STARED, stricken, and tried to make sense of this total incongruity. Tino was a demi-demonic human, a rare creature that had once been a man but since become endowed with infernal strength and frightening abilities. Not that Bernie had ever seen him be anything more than a public menace. She'd have chalked reports of demi power up to nothing more than fables and Order speculation if Dot hadn't told her otherwise. Even putting his objectively wicked nature aside, which should have barred him from an organization so steeped in puritanical trappings as the Temperance League, he was also the head of a bootlegging operation and the owner of a notorious nightclub.

What the hell was he doing here?

"Knight Chandler?"

Startled from her spiraling confusion, Bernie turned. A young woman wearing a blue and gold hijab and matching Temperance League sash stood behind her with a polite smile. One of the aides to the event organizers, she quickly introduced herself and explained she was to show Bernie to her seat if the Order had permitted her to take lunch with them.

Dazed and preoccupied, Bernie only nodded. She followed the aide as she led her to a round table near the edge of the ballroom. Other attendees were making their way to their seats now, too, and there was some activity around the raised platform at the head of the room.

"Here, Knight Chandler." The aide gestured to a chair. Bernie scanned the tabletop absently. Her gaze snagged on the name card next to her seat.

"Wait!" The aide paused from her retreat, surprised. "Pardon me, but… Is Mister Morandi to sit here as well?"

"Oh! Yes." She flashed Bernie a relieved smile. "We were so happy to find such a perfect seating solution. Mister Morandi is of course a very wealthy man, but, well, he isn't our normal type of donor. We are naturally well aware that Mister Morandi is a ward of the Order, and when the Order called asking for a seat, we surmised that you and he might have plenty to talk about over luncheon. Once the speeches are done, of course."

"Of course," Bernie repeated distantly, an impending sense of doom wrestling with cold anger under her skin.

The aide beamed. "Very good. We've had to accommodate so many last minute requests this year, it has truly been a feat to find proper seating for everyone. We hope you enjoy the luncheon, Knight Chandler!"

Bernie unbuckled her baldric, hung her sword over the chairback, and sat stiffly in her seat.

Through all the chatter, clinking of china, and drawing

back of chairs, she heard him approach. *Felt* him approach. Even before the scent of cigarettes reached her, she could feel a new tension thicken the air. Wherever he went, all eyes inevitably followed him. Some people quickly looked away, others gawked, and still others tried—and usually failed—to be coy about their surveillance of him. But they all looked. He was the closest thing to a demon they would ever see, just this side of "safe" while still radiating danger. Magic made flesh in a way they could only just understand. That perfect balance of known and unknown.

He knew it too. And he knew how to work it.

He paused, however, before sinking into the chair next to hers.

"Bernie."

"*Knight Chandler*," she corrected through clenched teeth.

He nodded to the other people seating themselves at the table. Two favored him with those carefully composed smiles that Old Money folk knew how to use as a sword and shield. The other two, New Money by the way they dressed, couldn't hide their interest.

"Funny, I thought that was your name, not mine."

She narrowed her eyes but refused to look at him. He knew what she meant. This was an old game they played, one that Bernie had never been fond of anyway.

"Seems ironic, letting a gin-peddler like you into a place like this."

He searched for an ashtray at the table. Finding none, he pinched the cigarette out between his fingers. If it burned, he didn't seem to care.

"Yeah, well, what can I say, I'm just a giving guy. Not very smart to say 'no' to the charitable type during a fundraiser, now, is it? Especially one as loaded as me."

Casually, he tucked the cigarette butt into his gold-plated, garnet studded cigarette case. To her immense relief, he didn't light up another.

On the stage, Ms. Káhtu Skenandoa, the celebrated leader of Chicago's Temperance League chapter, stepped regally up to the microphone and began welcoming the attendees to the Annual Autumn Fundraiser.

Bernie hardly listened. Tino made a good show of pretending to.

Finally, she could bite her tongue no longer.

"I didn't see you at the funeral," she said, keeping her voice low.

He shrugged, not even bothering to look at her.

"Had a feeling I wouldn't be too welcome."

"Oh, you had a feeling? That must have been a first."

He exhaled sharply through his nose, a dry, humorless sound.

"Look at that, two months later and you're already back to being a comedian."

Bernie's fingers closed into a fist on the tabletop as she fantasized about taking the dinner knife closest to her and burying it in Tino's heart, assuming he had one. Either way, demi that he was, he'd survive. But that would cause a scene, and anyway the crowd was clapping now, and Bernie followed along without knowing what she was clapping about. When the polite applause petered out, Bernie had regained enough self control to make a different observation, if not enough sense to leave well enough alone.

"I see you've put away your mourning blacks. If you ever put them on at all."

Finally, he settled his glowing eyes on her, a flash of impatience breaking through his smoothly smug mask.

"This is a treat, Bernie, truly, but let's cut the cute small talk. You're here on business, obviously." He raked a disdainful look over her. On the surface, he was referring to her uniform, but she knew what he was really implying: without it, her firmly middle class status would have barred her from entry to this ridiculous, hoity-toity nonsense. "You want the camera."

Surprise temporarily superseded her vitriol.

"Yes, but how did you–?"

"It's *my* business to know. And while *you* don't seem to have noticed, little no-rank that you are, you might find it handy to know you ain't the only one after it."

For the first time since clapping eyes on Tino, Bernie assessed the room. She frowned. She'd noticed the witches here and there, but now that everyone was locked by propriety into their seats instead of milling about, she had to admit there was a higher proportion attending than seemed usual, even in this day and age. And, as she scanned the tables, she noted how many of them were looking around too, searching the periphery of the event with sharp eyes and hardened faces.

"It's not just them."

Bernie started. Tino had leaned closer to her, his voice low. It made her skin crawl.

"See that guy over there? He works for Capone. And that ugly mug? Bugsie's boy. How much you wanna bet O'Banion sent someone, too?"

Bernie's palms began to sweat as she realized she had just stepped into something far bigger than she was prepared for or the Order understood.

"Good gravy. They all want the camera? Whyever for?"

Tino rolled his eyes. "Jesus Christ, they didn't tell you nothin' when they sent you here, did they?" He paused as the Old Money couple shot him a dirty look. He deftly hurled it back at them before continuing in a hiss, "That camera? The photographs it takes don't just show you. It shows your darkest secrets, too. And the useless fink using it is tryin' to blackmail half the people in here, only he's an idiot, so he's done it all wrong and painted a nice, bright target on his back."

Hell's hinges, this was getting messier and messier.

Bernie shook her head. "But I've been watching all the photographers here, none of them have a magic camera."

Tino gave her a withering, flat look. "Well, you must not have used that Oil right, because he's here. He just arrived later than the others."

"You seem terribly confident about that."

He tapped his temple, emphasizing his glowing eyes. "I've got better Second Sight than you'll ever have, even with that piss-weak potion you gals all tote around. I've seen him. He's here."

There was no reason not to believe that. It was a well-known fact that Tino had unparalleled Second Sight. That was one of the reasons the Order had given him the protection of Wardship. And one of the less obscure reasons they hadn't revoked it, despite all the trouble and heartache he'd caused.

"Where is he?"

Tino leaned away from her. "If he's smart, he's already flit. Don't think nobody else has quite zeroed in on him yet, though I could be wrong."

Bernie huffed, impatient. "Well, whatever did he look like?"

"Young. Gangly. Dark hair, dark eyes, bad suit. Egyptian maybe, or from somewhere thereabouts."

A cold stone dropped into Bernie's stomach, and more sweat broke out on her forehead and upper lip.

The boy. He'd taken her picture.

He'd taken *her* picture.

She should have touched up her Optical Oil sooner! If she had, she could have confiscated the camera then and there. Then she would be done. Then she wouldn't have to worry about…

Bernie struggled to swallow around the bile rising up her throat.

There was nothing for it now. She simply had to get to that camera before anyone else.

And, given all the other interested parties, she would need help. She was trained to face witches (she had some notable experience in that arena already), but she'd never faced so many at once. As for the mobsters, well, she normally carried a gun, but hadn't brought it with her today. The venue wouldn't allow it, though they'd been fine with the sword. Anyway, squaring up with mobsters was a whole 'nother world of complicated at the best of times. The Order and the gangs of Chicago afforded each other a wide berth, careful to pay each other the proper respect to avoid any conflict. But the Mob might be willing to kill for something like this. That camera presented all kinds of chilling opportunities to leverage power against just about anybody. Axing a single knight might be worth it, even if it did risk the Order's ire.

Yes, unfortunately, she needed help, and she needed it now.

Her voice came out surprisingly steady.

"We don't have time to lose. Tino, in the name of the Order I'm conscripting your services—"

He waved a hand. "Yeah, yeah, I figured a team-up was comin' from the moment I saw you sittin' there in that chair. So whaddaya got? What's the play?"

To her chagrin, her mind went utterly blank. In her year as a fully-inducted knight, Bernie had yet to handle a case this big. During her Squireship she had, but she'd had help; Dot had been her mentor, and Dot had a nose for trouble and a tendency to jump right into it. She'd been good at thinking on her feet. It was a talent Bernie still struggled to hone.

It occurred to her that Tino was relying on that ability, too. Of all the knights, almost all of which he categorically despised, he had worked most closely and consistently with Dot. He was used to her improvisations, her quick grasp of any situation and how to turn it in her favor, her uncanny ability to get the ball rolling. He must have assumed that Bernie shared the same skill.

She didn't. Not yet, at least.

"I—well..."

Another knight would be better suited for this. She should call the Order and inform them of the change in situation.

No, she couldn't. Time was of the essence, here. And–and the photograph…! They couldn't see the photograph.

Think.

"I saw him just before I saw you," Bernie said, and nodded in the direction he'd gone. "When was the last time you saw him?"

Tino shook his head, his mouth settling into a twist of frustration.

"Only caught a glimpse of him headin' in that same direction before I got shepherded over here. If I wasn't about to sit down, I woulda said 'to hell with it' and gone after him then and there."

"Why didn't you?"

"You were here. Didn't need Second Sight to tell you'd already seen me, the way you were sittin' here like you had a whole tree up your backside."

She sat up even straighter and turned to him. He was eying one set of mirrored doors along the western wall. Most of the photographers were being separated from their reporter partners busily jotting down notes on paper pads and herded into the corridor beyond. A few had been permitted to stay near the podium to take pictures of the speakers or remain on the balcony above.

Suddenly it made sense why he'd come here in the first place.

"You were after the camera, too. You wanted it for yourself!"

Of course he had. Having exclusive rights to a blackmail machine in Chicago? It could completely shift the balance of power. It could make an emperor out of a pauper. Tino was already a prince—which clearly wasn't enough for him.

He arched one dark brow at her, as if to say she should have already guessed as much. And she should have.

"Yeah, well, fat lot of good it is now, now that the Order's cottoned on to it." He huffed. "Best thing to do now is make sure it don't fall into any of my competition's hands."

Made sense enough. It was cold comfort, but it rang true. For reasons none of the lower knights really understood, Tino was beholden to the Order. Stealing that camera on the sly without the Order catching wise would be one thing. How could the Order be mad about a crime they knew nothing about? Stealing it in front of an Order knight was another. And while coven witches and gangsters might try to kill Bernie for the camera, Tino wouldn't. He was already on thin enough ice with the Order. If a knight were to come to harm by his hand, his life would be forfeit, and nothing, no law, no stretch of time or distance, would stop the Order from taking its justice.

That didn't mean she didn't have to stay sharp. If she happened to die incidentally in the course of their investigation, Tino would be off the hook.

It'd already happened that way once.

Bernie tightened her jaw. It wouldn't happen twice, not on her watch. Ready or not, she had to take control of this situation.

"You said you don't think anyone else knows who he is yet?"

He glanced around, his eyes tracking things she couldn't see, and shook his head.

"Not yet. But there's at least one spell in the works trying to sniff him out. And those gangsters won't have come alone. Probably got others stationed around the buildin', waitin' to follow anyone who looks likely."

Bernie nodded. "Well, it does seem like he's left the ballroom." She swore under her breath, earning another baleful look from their dining companions. "How are we going to find him?"

"His camera has a distinct magical signature. Makes… trails in the air. Like an afterimage. I can find him if we get a wiggle on."

"Then let's wiggle," Bernie said, rising in a single motion with Tino.

"Oh, how wonderful!" the speaker's voice boomed out from the stage. "Our first pledges!"

CHAPTER THREE

A SPOTLIGHT swiveled in their direction, pinning them to the spot, and a sea of faces turned in unison toward Bernie and Tino. For her part, Bernie was quite sure she was doing her best imitation of a boated fish, her eyes wide and her mouth opening and closing as her brain caught up with the sudden turn of events. She couldn't see Tino's reaction around the light beaming down on her face.

Polite applause fluttered up from the gathered socialites.

"Please, don't be shy!" Ms. Skenandoa crooned. "Come forward and start off our little fundraiser with a rousing speech!"

Bernie felt rooted to the spot. If she managed to make herself move, she was certain her feet would carry her in the opposite direction of the stage as fast as they could go. But Tino began weaving through the tables, and once he was a few steps ahead, her legs decided to unlock and follow him instead.

He took the steps up to the stage with surprising energy, and when he joined Skenandoa, he was wearing a broad, utterly charming smile. Skenandoa introduced him to the crowd, telling them his name before stumbling slightly when trying to find a way to describe his occupation without using the words "crime," "speakeasy," or "gin mill." She settled on calling him a business owner and associate of the Order before moving on to Bernie, whose introduction was much more straightforward and succinct–rather unfortunately, since Bernie was still desperately brainstorming what to say when the microphone was inevitably passed to her.

"Thank you, Káhtu," Tino said, shaking her hand before taking the microphone himself. "And thank you to everyone here for takin' the time to come to this event today and supportin' such a notable and noble cause."

He glanced over at Bernie and the corners of his mouth pulled pointedly wider, and Bernie realized hers were pressed into a line thin with worry. Taking his cue, she plastered a smile on her face. She was sure it looked nowhere near as genuine as his somehow did.

"I know the absolutely lovely Miss Skenandoa invited us to come up here and give everyone a rousing speech to help pry open those checkbooks–" a smattering of laughter followed that comment– "but I'm not the type to stand on ceremony, so I'll keep this short and sweet: my esteemed colleague has graciously given me the honor of announcing that The Order of Joan, whom I assist and serve with the greatest pleasure, is pledging to donate $2,500 to the Temperance League!"

A storm of applause greeted that proclamation. The smile Bernie was desperately maintaining wavered, and she imagined it had transformed into something closer to baring her teeth when Tino turned to look at her and clapped himself, looking oh-so-satisfied to find such a convenient way to inconvenience his handlers.

It was that look more than anything that wrenched Bernie firmly from the floaty, unreal feeling brought on by her fear of public speaking into that very real, very concrete moment where the rat bastard who couldn't even be bothered to show up to Dot's funeral was taking an extra dig at the institution that had employed her, the same one that *still* offered him protections and privileges in exchange for his unique services, which were only barely enough to outweigh the fact that he was an absolute, unrepentant *son of a bitch* who cared for nothing and no one beyond himself, anyway.

And suddenly, she was taking the microphone from him and speaking through the biggest, most camera-friendly smile there ever was.

"Thank you, thank you," she cooed to the crowd as the applause began to subside. "And thank you, Mister Morandi. He really was so excited by the opportunity to represent the Order's charity and esteem for the Temperance movement at this Luncheon today. But I'm the one who has truly been given the gift here, because Mister Morandi–" she glanced at him, smiling sweetly, and was pleased to see his own smile had stiffened, "– ever the gentleman, has given me the honor of announcing his own commitment to personally donate double the value of the Order's pledge today!"

The diners erupted into greater applause, some rising to their feet.

"That's right! $5,000 dollars, ladies and gentlemen, courtesy of Mister Morandi!"

She stepped back as the ovation continued, falling in beside Tino as photographers converged on the stage, the bright pop of their flashbulbs pelting them. Skenandoa, as shocked as everyone else by this unpredicted turn of events, gushed into the microphone about their generosity, clearly flustered and flushed with breathless excitement.

They posed politely for a few seconds, each wearing their best smiles before Tino broke their stance, waved to the audience and Skenandoa, and beat feet off the stage. Bernie followed him as they wound through the tables.

"Well played," he snapped in a low voice. "Shoulda known better than to play a trick like that with you. Every time we cross paths, you always gotta be a pain in my ass."

Bernie smirked silently, relishing in the satisfaction of the moment.

"You started it, I ended it." The smirk slipped away as she contemplated having to explain to her Matron why the Temperance League suddenly expected them to fork over 2,500 bucks.

"Yeah, well, great fuckin' job wastin' more of our time on that stage at my expense, because the trail is fadin'. We gotta move fast now." He pointed to a door as they bypassed their seats, Bernie plucking her sword from her chairback as Tino snatched his hat from his. A man wearing the hotel's uniform was standing in front of it.

"We gotta get through there," he went on, settling his hat on his head. "Since you just put me out five grand, I'm not in the bribing mood. Flash him some gam or your badge, whichever gets us through faster."

Bernie scowled. She didn't need a badge, and she certainly didn't need to show some leg: the Order coat and sword were enough, typically. He should know the ins and outs of how this all worked, considering how often he'd worked with Dot. Besides, the man Tino had indicated wasn't acting as a security guard; he was simply a hotel employee manning the door to make sure nobody ended up in the hotel's service areas.

"Good afternoon," she said as they neared, "I'm Knight-Maiden Bernice Chandler, on business with the Order of Joan. We need to go through this door."

The young man took in her sword and coat at a glance and stepped aside. "Of course."

She started forward, then stopped.

"Has anybody else been through here?"

He gave her a mildly confused look. "Why, the staff, naturally."

"Naturally. Anybody else?"

He started to shake his head, to say "no," but Tino interjected.

"How much did the kid with the camera slip ya?"

The other man's discomfort deepened as he finally took more than passing note of Tino. "I'm sure I don't know—"

He stuttered to a stop as Tino tipped down his glasses, exposing his lurid, glowing, definitely not human eyes.

"You might wanna work on lying better before Bugsy's boys come over here askin' the same thing. They ain't gonna play as nice."

He paled to an almost frightening pallor as he glanced between Tino's preternatural eyes and the crowd behind them.

"I—he—ten dollars."

Bernie's jaw dropped. That was an exorbitant amount. "Just to get through?"

"N-no. He entered this way, too. And he wanted to use the staff restrooms to change for the event."

Bernie thanked the man in passing and moved on, her mind racing ahead as she and Tino started down the service corridor, dodging curious employees as they went. So the boy had entered in street clothes—which meant he would probably leave in street clothes. That would help shake off anybody looking for a photographer dressed for a swanky event. Tino seemed to be thinking the same thing.

"Kid's the smart kinda stupid. Smart enough to be a problem, stupid enough not to realize how utterly fucked he is, squeezin' down the kind of people he's squeezin'."

The service corridors were a maze, but Tino navigated down them with ease, following something Bernie couldn't see. The headache lurking behind her eye was steadily throbbing, and she still hadn't had the opportunity to put another drop in. They passed a restroom, and the way Tino's eyes lingered on its door before forging ahead suggested the photographer had already come and gone.

He couldn't be that far ahead of them, could he? Bernie

wondered as Tino waved off a hotel clerk who tried to intercept them. How far could he have gone? And how long did it take to develop film anyway? Her hand, already resting on her sword's pommel, gripped it tighter. She had to get the negative *before* it was developed into a photograph. If he developed it... if he saw—

Tino came to a door, pushed it open, and stopped abruptly. Bernie, distracted, ran into him. She spluttered, about to scold him, when she caught sight of what had drawn him up short.

The door opened onto a service alley, and it was full of people. People, and motion, and sound, and *magic*. She couldn't see the magic flying through the air without the Optical Oil, but she could feel it. The protective bracelet of crystals and nazars around her wrist had flushed with heat, warming her skin to an uncomfortable degree.

Peering over Tino's shoulder, her eyes widened. There were at least nine people from three distinct covens fighting each other. One man was opening his mouth to recite a spell, but a woman spat something in a foreign language and made a rapid gesture with her hand, and the words the man said next were jumbled, totally nonsensical, rendering his casting useless. A man in a flat-cap joined the fray wielding a nightstick, only instead of hauling off to strike his opponents, he merely tapped them. Whatever limb the weapon touched seemed to instantly lose function. In less than a second, two people had collapsed to the ground on numb legs, and a third had dropped the fan she was using for... something magical that they'd arrived too late to see.

All this ground to a halt as every eye in the alleyway turned to the open door and the two of them framed by it, Bernie in her bright Order overcoat and Tino with his glowing eyes.

And every eye that turned to them began making rapid calculations.

If they attacked Bernie, they'd risk the Order's ire… but it might be worth it to get their hands on something so powerfully useful.

Tino was trickier. All the covens knew he was something special, had heard rumors that magic didn't stick to him quite as it should, but none of them knew how true any of the stories were and to what extent.

"Valentino," one of the witches greeted frostily.

"Mildred," he said in an answering rumble.

The tension in the air drew tighter.

Gathering her courage, Bernie cleared her throat and stepped fully out into the alley.

"Knight Chandler, Order of Joan." She made a point of surveying the people gathered. "Is there a problem here?"

Behind her, Tino shifted and whispered, "Bernie."

She glanced over her shoulder. Tino twitched his head toward a trash can to their left. An old suit, the same suit Bernie had seen the young photographer wearing, lay crumpled atop the garbage, confirming her earlier suspicions.

Clever. Whether the boy knew that ditching his clothes could shrug off several kinds of tracking spells was as yet unconfirmed, but she suspected more and more that he wasn't a complete rube when it came to magic.

The woman Tino had called Mildred, a stately dark-skinned and round-faced witch, spoke up.

"This is coven business," she announced, a warning lurking beneath the words. "There is no need or place for the Order here."

"I disagree," countered Bernie with a forced smile, her grip tightening on her sword pommel. "I am here by coven invitation to investigate a magical object."

The assembled practitioners exchanged significant looks. They reached some silent agreement.

Having already taken the initiative, Mildred spoke again.

"Whatever your investigation, it doesn't concern us. We know nothing about any magical object, and there are no mundies in the vicinity to be hurt, which means we can do as we will. So, I'll say it again, knight: *this is coven business*. It doesn't concern you."

Ah. That was how they were going to play this: deny any knowledge of the camera, then if Bernie intervened and got burned, claim she interfered in their affairs without cause.

In other words: get lost, or get hurt.

Bernie had no intention of getting caught up in a fight. She had every intention of pursuing the photographer, though, and they couldn't afford to lose the trail Tino was following. They had to cross through the alleyway.

Carefully, she removed her hand from her sword pommel.

"I see. We'll just show ourselves to the street, then," she said, hoping that might quell their rising ire, if not their suspicions.

Tino snorted. "Yeah, that'll work."

She wanted to shoot him a look because *that* comment definitely wasn't going to help, but instead directed a reassuring smile at the assembly.

Unfortunately, she hadn't smiled much in the last few months, and the product was painfully wooden.

A current went through the practitioners, subtle but palpable, and Bernie's hopes withered.

Tino reached up to loosen his tie and fiddled with the underlying collar bar. Casually, he announced, "Before we get started, you should know: I can't hurt normies—they're too soft, haven't got a snowball's chance in hell of defending themselves from the likes of me. But according to the Order, you bunch with your magic that *might* leave a scuff or two, if you throw the first punch…" He paused and smiled. It was cold and sharp, and there was nothing forced about *his*. "You're fair game."

Nobody moved, the covens silently negotiating who would make the opening gambit. Bernie almost missed the twitch of movement from the man carrying the nightstick. He leapt toward her, the baton a black blur as he swung for her arm. She twisted, drawing her sword partially from its sheath. The nightstick met the blade's exposed edge and sheared smoothly in two, the top half falling to her feet and skittering across the grimy alleyway concrete. She shifted again, taking advantage of his momentary surprise, and thrust the sword pommel into his nose with a sharp crunch. He reeled back with a howl, granting her room to finish drawing her sword.

The tension snapped, and the violence held in check exploded forth.

Another of the flat-cap gang, a member of the Brotherhood of Simon Magus, lunged at her wielding a silvered cane. Its magical properties must have been more formidable than the nightstick's, because her Order sword didn't instantly cut through it. Green sparks fountained out where their weapons met, hot pinpricks stinging where they fell on Bernie's skin. The Brother bore down on her, eyes slit against the bright shower of sparks. Behind her, she heard a startled cry followed by a heavy impact against brick, but she couldn't look to see what Tino was doing without glancing over her shoulder. The Brother did, his attention reflexively caught by the flash of sound and movement. Bernie pushed him off balance, then kicked his leg out from under him as he stumbled. He barely had time to yelp before his face smacked the concrete, and his silver cane flew from his hand.

A third Brother appeared at her shoulder, crowbar raised. Bernie parried the first blow. The second never came. She slipped past his guard and thrust the tip of her sword into the meaty flesh where his arm met his shoulder, striking bone. He dropped his weapon with a sharp cry and clapped a hand over the wound. It wasn't mortal, but it would make a nasty scar and an aching injury in cold snaps to come.

Another shout and impact drew her attention, just in time to see a woman sliding down the alley's opposite wall and landing in a heap on the ground, alive but clearly dazed. From the corner of her eye, she noticed Mildred engaged with another practitioner. She and Tino hadn't become the sole targets as she'd feared, but simply been absorbed into the inter-coven brawl.

Mildred briefly caught Bernie's eye. She spat, "Get out of here, knight!" at the same time Tino said, "We don't have time for this, Bernie." He yanked her around by the shoulder, pointing her toward the alley's mouth.

She jerked her shoulder out from under his hand. What did he think she was doing, just funning around? Nevermind the small part of her that chafed at being pulled away from the action, that reveled in the singular kind of focus a good fight required. A good fight could hammer unruly emotions into a sharp blade as surely as a smith could hot iron, and Bernie had a lot of unruly emotions of late.

But her sense won out. She started toward the street, dodging wild blows and stumbling bodies. It seemed a few more practitioners had appeared in the brief minute she'd been engaged, and there were probably more on the way.

They were nearing the alley's mouth when the woman with the fan caught up to them. Numb arm still dangling, she had retrieved her weapon and now wielded it in her other hand, sending concentrated gusts of force over the fray with controlled flicks of her wrist, clearing her path to them. Bernie noticed her only a moment before she aimed a gust at them and barely had time to jump aside. She staggered as the blast buffeted her into the alley wall. Her shoulder met the rough brick with bruising force.

Tino got the brunt of it. It had as much success moving him as wind would a brick wall. It broke off him in a sudden burst of flames, tongues flaring bright and hot as the fan's magic reacted with his own. The backdraft sent his hat flying off his head, and a wave of heat flushed across Bernie. The scent of singed cloth and burning trash filled the air; a nearby stack of packing crates waiting to be collected had caught fire.

The woman with the fan paled as smoke rapidly began to fill the alley. Tino glowered at her and took a step in her direction.

But the woman cried out a moment later as one of Mildred's women grabbed her arm and twisted it viciously.

Bernie and Tino both took the opportunity to turn tail and rush for the street.

"We need to get out of here, fast!" Bernie coughed, the smoke stinging her eyes.

"I'm on it," Tino answered. They burst onto the busy sidewalk, blinking in the brighter light, though the day was overcast. Curiously, there was no crowd of anxious spectators peering at the spectacle occurring in the alleyway. Bernie wondered wildly why until she noticed a series of hastily scrawled text in chalk on either side of the alley, some kind of attention deflection spell. But the smoke was beginning to attract notice.

Fast-approaching footfalls sent another bolt of adrenaline through Bernie, and she started running down the sidewalk. The nazar bracelet around her wrist was growing hot again, indicating gathering magic, and with how fast it was heating, she had no doubt it was targeted at her.

"There!" Tino shouted suddenly, pointing at a Dodge sedan further up the street. He charged forward, reaching it before Bernie. He wrenched the door open and slid across the bench seat to the driver's side, effortlessly popping the dash plate out. Bernie dove in after him and looked back just in time to see one of the Brotherhood surging out of the alley behind them, coughing and waving the smoke away from his face as he searched.

He spotted them.

"Tino," Bernie warned, watching as the man, heedless of the bewildered pedestrians gawking at the smoke and shouting for the fire brigade, wound up to cast a hex.

The engine coughed, then roared to life. With a squeal of tires and a mighty lurch that nearly slung Bernie back out onto the sidewalk cement, they were off. The passenger side door lolled open, and Bernie seized it as they careened down State Street, but it wouldn't latch. Belatedly, she realized the demon beside her had broken the mechanism and she'd have to hold it closed herself if she didn't want it to fly open and slam into other cars or, God forbid, people.

And that was looking ever more likely as Tino wove through traffic, ignoring signs, signals, and traffic police alike. Horns blared, other motorists yelled, people screamed.

"Slow down!" Bernie shouted, eyes wide with horror as they swerved around a truck full of oranges with a hair's breadth of clearance.

"Can't!" he shouted back. "We're being followed!"

She didn't want to take her eyes off the road in front of them, but she did. And Tino was right: two more cars were streaking through the wake of the chaos Tino was wreaking.

"The covens?" Bernie asked, turning her attention forward again and flinching as they narrowly avoided another collision. As quickly as she could, she braced her sword between her knees and struggled to find purchase on the paltry lip of the dash for extra stability.

"Gangs. Musta caught sight of the ruckus, seen you, and realized we were after the same thing they are." They blasted through an intersection. He glanced down the cross street before saying, "Hold on, we gotta lose 'em."

Then he pushed the pedal to the floor.

Bernie screamed, her knuckles pale against the door and dashboard.

Tino laughed, white teeth flashing, grinning ear to ear like a kid at a carnival.

They surged through the traffic, swerving madly, turning down a dizzying tangle of streets. Heart galloping and stomach roiling, Bernie squeezed her eyes shut. An endless cacophony of blaring horns, screeching tires, shouts, crunching metal and shattering glass trailed them.

And then, just when she thought she really might upchuck all over the dash, they slowed.

Cautiously, she dared to peek at the world outside. It was no longer flying by in a jerky, impressionistic whirl. They were coasting down a residential street, autumn-bare trees lining its sidewalks. Somewhere in the distance police sirens howled, but this neighborhood seemed peaceful, all things considered. People chatted with each other from their stoops, stomping their feet and rubbing their hands together to keep warm. Kids ran between the houses in whooping packs, their breaths coming out in white clouds. A barking dog loped at their heels, determined not to be left out of the fun.

"We lost 'em," Tino said, guiding them down the sleepier street at a much more reasonable speed. "You can stop putting scratches in the finish now."

CHAPTER FOUR

BERNIE LOOSENED her grip on the door. Her hands were shaking. She was shaking. She'd rather fight a whole coven of angry witches than go on another joy ride with Tino.

"Park. Now," she managed, trying to sound authoritative. It came out breathless.

He darted a disdainful look over her.

"Fine. Was about to anyway."

They coasted up to a free bit of curbside real estate. The passenger side door listed open once released, and Bernie tumbled out onto the sidewalk, barely keeping her legs beneath her. The air she pulled into her lungs was icy. She hated the cold with a passion. She focused on that instead of the vaguely sick sensation still rolling around her middle, and that seemed to do the trick. By the time Tino had exited the car and rounded the hood to stand beside her, she could straighten up without feeling like she was out at sea.

"What," she started, and was satisfied to hear her voice no

longer shook, "in God's name was *that*?" Now that she no longer felt like puking, the smoldering coals of her hatred for the man beside her had room to flare up, bright and hot.

Tino shrugged, not even doing her the courtesy of looking her in the eye. Instead, he was scanning the street and surrounding houses, hardly a hair out of place.

"Drivin'. You could learn to yourself if you could afford a car."

"*Driving*? Are you completely deranged? You could have gotten us killed!" she seethed, barely controlling the wild desire to scream at him at the top of her lungs, to grab hold of him and shake him like a rag doll or sock him hard in the nose. "You could have killed somebody! You might have, from all the collisions I heard behind us!"

"I didn't," he said with perfect conviction. "So what's there to complain about? You're alive, ain't ya? In one piece? And we ain't got nobody tailin' us now, do we? Come on," he started down the sidewalk, shoving his hands in his trouser pockets. His overcoat was still in the coat-check at the Blackstone; he only had his dinner jacket to keep him warm. Unlike her, the cold didn't seem to faze him one bit. "Camera's this way."

The last thing she wanted to do was go anywhere with him. But he walked with purpose, and she recalled with a jolt of dread the camera, the photograph of her, and her mission.

"You know where to go?" she asked grudgingly once she caught up with him.

He nodded. "Saw the trail goin' this way when we passed the first time. Had to shake the goons off, though, before we could double back. Looks like the signature ends up there."

Ahead of them, a row of modest apartment buildings rose, each three stories tall, each a block of warm, earthy red against the cold gray sky. The one Tino seemed bound for lacked adornment but was well maintained, a nice place for working class families to call home.

They entered, warmth and the smell of myriad herbs and spices washing over them. Tino paused in the modest lobby, glancing first up the stairs and then to a hallway that led further back into the building. After a moment of indecision, he clenched his jaw and bypassed the stairway into the narrow corridor.

Bernie followed, grateful to be out of the October chill, anxious to find the camera and put this whole nightmare behind her. As it was, she'd have a mountain of paperwork to fill out once she returned to Headquarters, and she was sure her Knight-Matron would want a full report…

The staccato sound of a lock breaking brought her fully back to the present. Tino shoved open the door—the second door he'd broken in less than an hour—and descended down a series of steps into the building's basement.

Bernie froze in the doorway, suddenly paralyzed. If there was something she hated worse than cold, it was basements.

A shiver of fear ran through her, wild and irrepressible. She closed her eyes, pushed it away. Six years, she told herself, was a long time, long enough to conquer her fear of basements even if she couldn't yet forget it.

God, how she wished she could forget it.

She forced herself to take the first step, then the next and the next.

Tino hadn't waited for her at the bottom, where the stairwell opened up into a wider, longer room. It was almost entirely filled by a forest of pipes, dimly illuminated by bare bulbs every six feet or so. Four doors interrupted the masonry on the right-hand wall, and Tino was already forcing his way into the third one down, breaking yet another lock and adding another form to the mountain of paperwork waiting for Bernie later; the Order was responsible for the replacement cost of any damage Tino left in his wake. But of course *Tino* wasn't the one who was going to have to total it up and report it to her superiors, so he didn't care. In fact, she suspected he was doing it on purpose. Seemed like a pretty reckless thing to do, considering how furious everyone was with him at Order Headquarters. But then, Tino never really did seem to care much about the Order.

He'd *seemed* to care an iota for Dot, and look where that had gotten her?

Grinding her teeth, Bernie hurried after him, ignoring the cold sweat that had broken out on her face. Red light emanated from the open doorway, along with the sound of Tino shuffling about inside.

He was hunched over a stack of developed photographs, one of nearly a dozen spread out across multiple surfaces. This room had once been a maintenance worker's office, she realized, before it had been completely converted into a dark room. Clotheslines crisscrossed the space, and drying photographs hung from them like pendants on banners, images of people she didn't know captured in stark black and white staring out at her. Wealthy, all of them, some haughty, some jovial.

And behind every single one danced a ghostly image.

The man grinning around a cigar was flanked by a faint, pale reflection of himself, naked and entangled with another man. A young woman fresh from the dance floor at some evening event was haunted by the phantom image of a child. Over another woman's shoulder hovered a small medicine bottle and a bowl of porridge. She was conversing with a man with three ephemeral wedding rings floating above his head.

A bloodied bat. A case of money. A ship. A letter. Image after image developed, secret after secret exposed, some more cryptic than others.

What would hers look like?

Behind the thicket of hanging photographs, she spied shallow dishes waiting along the workbench spanning the far wall, bottles of chemicals lined up next to them. If the film had been developed, it would be somewhere back there.

Tino continued to rifle through the developed pictures with a look of fierce determination.

"Stop that," she snapped, starting toward the workbench. "We need to find the camera, not dig up dirt on your business associates." She pushed aside row after row of low-hanging banners filled with unfamiliar faces, each step bringing her heart one inch higher in her throat. The sounds of Tino's search didn't stop, but before she could comment again, she caught sight of it: a coat hanger dangling from the workbench's pegboard, black strands of film clipped to its bottom wire. They glistened in the red light, damp from their chemical bath and dripping onto the countertop.

An invisible hand tightened around her throat. It was everything she could do not to run over to them and seize them immediately. She forced herself to approach with measured steps, lest Tino notice and question her about her interest. In her ears, her heartbeat drummed.

Gingerly, she unclipped a strand of film and held it up to the red light.

Yes, these were from the Temperance Luncheon. She recognized a few faces, did her best not to notice the ghostly images of their secrets hovering just over their shoulders. The strand she held didn't include her likeness. Rather than waste any more time hunting for it, she grabbed the other two strands and shoved all three into her inner coat pocket, dampness be damned. Her hands shook as she withdrew them.

"Tino," she repeated, "look around for the camera."

"It isn't here," he said, distracted. "It's upstairs."

Bernie rounded on him, where he was pawing through another pile of prints.

"Then what are we—?"

He had taken his sunglasses off, and his preternaturally golden eyes were bright in the red glow as they darted between one photograph and the next. There was a feverish kind of gleam to them, and a fervent edge to every move he made.

"He took your photograph," Bernie stated, and oh, of course, it made so much sense! He might have wanted the camera—useful tool that it was—but his real goal in coming to the Luncheon hadn't been to steal it; it'd been to find the photographer and secure his picture. If all he'd wanted was the camera, he might have given Bernie the slip back at the Blackstone. What he'd said had been true, to a certain extent: he didn't want the camera falling into the wrong hands, for more reasons than one. But the photograph had been his primary concern, retrieving it his first priority. Bernie, and by extension the Order, was a means to that end; the authority granted to her provided a potential leg up for him in this race for the ultimate prize. And if everything went sideways, well, the Order had forgiven him many transgressions already. Perhaps he believed they might forgive him one more. That's why he'd teamed up with her. He was protecting himself.

She could only imagine what horrible secrets held in the depths of his black heart the camera's magic had exposed.

Dispensing with combing through the stacks in an orderly fashion, Tino swept them out over the tabletop, pushing them around, revealing face after face that wasn't his.

"It's gotta be here somewhere," he growled. "Where the fuck is it?"

His movements grew more erratic. Photographs began slipping off the tables and scattering across the floor.

Faces peered up at Bernie from the floor in bits and pieces, the squares of photosensitive paper overlapping each other. In amongst the jigsaw of lips, hair, noses, and cheeks, she spied the bright ring of a familiar eye.

She hesitated. Yes, she despised Tino. Yes, she was curious.

But she had her own secrets she was protecting; didn't he have a right to do the same for his?

But then she remembered her mentor, and her untimely death, and Tino's questionable role in it. Her decision was made in a heartbeat.

While Tino continued to tear through the other photographs, she knelt and plucked his up from the gritty cement floor.

She lifted it, and looked at it, and frowned.

It had been taken at some dinner party. The room was full of people, each and every one with a flute of champagne or some other drink in hand. No one was looking directly into the camera except Tino.

Tino, his image captured in a parting of the crowd, his distinctive eyes intent as he stared into the lens, as if he'd known it was there. He was not smiling. He was not frowning in confusion, as she imagined he might in that moment between recognizing the signature of strange magic and the closing of the shutter, sealing his likeness inside.

He was looking directly at the camera, expressionless, except for his eyes. His eyes, which always burned.

And the space around him was clear, devoid of anything but traces of the cigarette smoke hanging over the partygoers.

Devoid of secrets.

It was just him and the camera.

Bernie's brow wrinkled. How could that be? But then she recalled one of the most notable aspects of demies: magic didn't always work on them the same way it did on everybody else.

A hot spike of jealousy lanced through Bernie unexpectedly.

Tino's secrets, no matter how dark, no matter how painful, were safe.

The bitterness of it all almost choked her.

"Tino," she breathed. The flurry of shoe-soles scraping against cement and paper sliding over paper instantly ceased. In two strides he was in front of her. He snatched the photograph roughly from her hands.

He stared at it, his expression as blank as the one in his photograph, except there was a palpable sense of expectation beneath it. A hunger, even.

She watched his golden demon eyes search the photograph and find nothing.

Dawning comprehension settled over him. Any moment now his shoulders would relax and he would smile, probably joke about how untouchable he was.

That wasn't what happened. Or, not exactly. He did start laughing, but it was strange. It didn't sound relieved; it sounded disappointed. And it kept going, growing louder, like he'd just heard the most ridiculous joke in the world. Unaccountably disturbed, Bernie took a step back without thinking. Tino shook his head and looked up.

"Of course!" he said to the ceiling, his harsh, caustic laughter fading. He ran a hand down his face, where his palm stopped to cup his mouth. From beneath it, she heard, "Nearly had me there, didn't You?"

With a flick of his wrist, he tossed the photograph away. It flipped through the air and slipped across the others littering the floor like too-big confetti, finally lodging up against one leg of the workbench.

When she returned her attention to him, the lines of his face had smoothed. He slipped on his glasses, the dark lenses hiding the damning evidence of his true nature, and he smiled at her, broad and unfriendly, like he always did.

"Let's go get that fuckin' camera."

Bernie only nodded, as unable to find the words to ask him what had just happened as she was to find a care to say them. The demi turned and strode out the door, one last chuckle bubbling out of him. With a final pat of her coat front, confirming the presence of the damp film hidden in the pocket underneath, Bernie struck out after him, ready to bring this mission to an end.

CHAPTER FIVE

WHEN THEY arrived at the door of the photographer's apartment on the second floor, Bernie stopped Tino.

"Let me handle this," she told him. He looked like his usual self now, dark-tinted glasses as firmly in place as his unflappable persona, but his brief episode in the basement had given her pause. An extra dose of caution, she thought, was well-warranted.

Though, after another moment of consideration, she realized even under the best circumstances she wouldn't let him do the talking for something like this.

She knocked. Within the apartment, a set of footsteps approached the door.

A young woman wearing a burgundy hijab and a floral kitchen apron opened it wide. Her casual curiosity became surprise when she took in Bernie's persimmon overcoat.

"Yes?"

Bernie gave her a reassuring smile.

"Good afternoon, Miss. I'm Knight-Maiden Bernice

Chandler. This is my," she tried to think of a good word to describe her current relationship with Tino—and then wondered if she shouldn't have asked him to post up somewhere else, considering how recognizable his name was, if not his face—and settled on, "assistant. We're with the Order of Joan. Would you mind if I asked you some questions?"

Bewildered, the young woman looked between them. "Of course."

"Does a young man live here? A photographer?"

As soon as Bernie mentioned photography, the woman's face fell.

"What did he do this time?" Then, more anxious, "Is he in trouble?"

Bernie measured her next words.

"He may be. More importantly, he may be in danger."

At that, the woman paled.

"What kind of danger? Does this have something to do with all the money?"

"Yeah," Tino said laconically, "it has to do with that. Takin' pictures of celebrities don't normally pay that much, doll."

The woman turned her wide, brown eyes on Tino. She frowned. Bernie clenched her teeth and resisted the urge to elbow Tino hard in the ribs.

"I-I thought that it didn't," she admitted, "but he said… and—Well, why are you here?" She examined Bernie's overcoat and sword again, perplexed and uneasy.

"The camera your brother—" Bernie had guessed their relation to each other accurately, given the woman's lack of reaction, "—uses is magical in nature. He's upset a lot of very powerful people. We may be able to help with that. May we come in?"

A new expression passed across the woman's face, there and gone in a flash. It held recognition, Bernie thought, and fear. The woman hesitated. From somewhere deeper in the apartment, a small voice cried, "Sissy!" and the scent of burning food wafted out the door.

Indecision gave way to resignation. She stepped back from the door.

"Come in," she said, and retreated back into the apartment, hurrying to the kitchen.

Gray smoke was rising from a pan on the kitchen stove. Two young boys and a girl, all under the age of ten, sat around a table set for a late lunch. There was no sign of the photographer, but judging from the way Tino's eyes lingered on the hallway leading into the apartment's more private rooms, he was likely somewhere back there. A soft hissing sound emanated from the kitchen's far wall, water running through pipes. He was in the shower then.

One of the boys, the eldest of the three, had just removed the pan from its burner. He paused when he saw them.

"Fatima, who are they?"

"Guests," she answered, taking the pan from him. "Mind your manners." She turned back to Bernie and Tino. "Samir should be out any moment now."

"May I ask you a few questions in the meantime?"

Fatima sighed as she scraped the ruined dish into the trash.

"Sure. What do you want to know?"

Bernie asked when Samir obtained the camera. He had many cameras, Fatima answered. Photography had been a long time hobby of Samir's. But the one she suspected they were searching for he had inherited a year ago, upon their father's death. Their father had been a watchmaker, she went on. He'd made good money, but he'd had debts, and his death threatened to tumble what was left of their family into poverty. Their mother had died shortly after their sister's birth, and so they had no one left to support them. The super of this small building had taken pity on their family and made Samir his assistant, while Fatima occasionally made money by supplying daycare for other neighborhood families. But still, they struggled. Then, a few months ago, Samir had started bringing more money home than he could possibly be making from his day job.

"He told me he'd taken up photography, and that people were paying him to take their pictures." She shrugged, and Bernie noticed the dark bags under her eyes in the better light coming through the windows. "I didn't question him. We needed the money."

Boy, did Bernie know how that felt.

"And where did your father get the camera—?" Bernie started to ask, but a burst of noise interrupted her. Samir, freshly showered and changed, had been returning to the kitchen for lunch. Upon catching sight of them, he immediately bolted back toward his room.

"Oh no you don't!" Tino said. With frightening speed and efficiency, he grabbed Samir by the collar, hauled him into the kitchen, and kicked a chair out from the table. He threw the young man into it with so much force Samir nearly tumbled backward, chair and all.

"Sit down, kid. Stay a spell. Tell us what kinda moron are you, to bring this shit into your own fuckin' house." Tino's voice sharpened as he loomed over him, the threat of imminent violence obvious in his posture. "Straight to your family's front door, no less. You stupid little—"

"Tino, that's enough!" Bernie shouted, alarmed. The three children were staring at Tino, wide-eyed and open-mouthed, their hands reaching for each other's. Fatima, gripping her iron pan tightly, had started to wind up to swing at Tino, but held off when Bernie intervened.

Scowling, Tino backed away from Samir, and Fatima, still eying him warily, loosened her grip on the pan but didn't set it down.

Bernie let everyone take a deep breath. Lord knew she needed one.

"I'm sorry for my associate's actions, truly," Bernie said, glancing reproachfully at Tino, "but we really do have reason to believe you could be in danger. All of you. And we need answers before we can help you."

There was a general pause. The children hugged each other, confused as their little eyes darted between the gathered adults. Samir was pale, watching Tino with a sheen of terror glazing his eyes. From the anger continuing to gather around Fatima like a heavy atmosphere, Bernie was sure she would turn Bernie and Tino out at any moment, and she'd be fully in her rights to do so.

But then she turned her ire on her brother, a rapid patter of blistering words spoken in their mother tongue hurled at him from across the kitchen table. Bernie knew enough Arabic to catch some of it, and was impressed by Fatima's skillful use of colorful swears.

"Alright, alright!" Samir yelped finally. "I'll cooperate, I'll tell them what they want to know!"

Hearing this, Tino abandoned the station he'd taken up by Samir's seat to thwart any attempts at escape. Casting a dark look over his shoulder, he stalked over to the windows, twitching back the curtains to observe the street below.

In his seat, Samir relaxed a fraction. He ran a shaking hand through his damp black hair. Still, when he finally met Bernie's eye, he mustered a half-smile and said, "Well, well. I guess we meet again, beautiful."

Bernie raised one eyebrow. "We do at that, though regrettably not under the best of circumstances."

The little grin faded. He nodded.

"How did you find me? I thought—"

"You thought you shook off all the spells and trackers?" Bernie shrugged. "You did an impressive job, all things considered. But the Order has its ways."

Samir glanced nervously at Tino, who remained by the window unmoving, by all accounts focused solely on the world outside.

"Tell us about the camera. Please."

Samir looked back at Bernie. His lips narrowed, pinched.

She sighed.

"The jig is up, Samir," Bernie stated. "The covens and gangs are catching wise, and the Order is now involved. You've made a lot of very powerful people very angry. It's time to come clean and give it up. If you do, the Order can protect you."

When he still hesitated, Fatima answered.

"It was our Baba's. He bequeathed it to Samir when he died, but there was a letter with it. He warned us never to use it." She shot Samir a withering glare at that.

"Did he say why?"

Now Fatima hesitated. "He—"

"Fatima!"

"Didn't you hear them, Sammy?" she spat at her brother. "You've angered the wrong people! They'll find you soon, and then they'll find us. If you love your family, you will tell them what it is. And if you don't, you can leave right now and I will tell them."

Chastened, Samir slumped back in his chair, arms crossed moodily. His younger sister, no more than five, whimpered before the first big tears began to roll down her face. Fatima finally relinquished the pan in her hand and swept her younger sister up in an embrace, patting her back soothingly.

"I was just trying to help us. It wasn't enough, what Mister Rinaldi was paying. You know that."

His sister shook her head. "I know that, *khouya*. But that doesn't matter now. It's over. Tell them about the camera."

He took a deep breath and met Bernie's eyes.

"The camera has a djinni inside."

It was all Bernie could do not to gasp, but she could not help how her eyes bugged. Tino's gaze snapped from the street below to the photographer at the table, his backbone straightening like he'd just been delivered a powerful shock. He examined Samir with closer, narrow-eyed scrutiny.

A djinn? How? Who would have the skill to put a djinni, an elemental, a being of first-degree magic, in a camera? Who would be mad enough to do such a thing? And why?

"Our Baba practiced 'Ilm al-Limiya." He mistook Bernie's continued awestruck silence for ignorance and explained, "He was a sorcerer who could harness the power of higher beings. In his letter, he explained that during the war, when Fatima and I were small and we still lived in Egypt, he'd been recruited by the Turks to bind djinn into objects. It was highly experimental work, and dangerous. The Ottomans were trying to find more ways to contain djinn and control their power, to put their magic to new uses. The camera was one of their successes, a device of our father's own design. He wrote that it was used for espionage."

"Jesus Christ," Tino growled. Glowering, he turned away and resumed his vigil, his arms crossed and his shoulders tense.

Bernie fought to find words.

"Y–you knew all that and you still decided to… to *use* it?"

He shrugged, cross, and jerked his chin toward his younger siblings. "I thought that was the preferable option to dropping Magdi, Gamal, and Khadiga off at the orphanage. Don't you?"

She wasn't sure how to answer that, probably because there wasn't a good answer. Binding djinn against their will was never a good idea, and she had no reason to believe the one in the camera had volunteered. Their father's warning against using the camera suggested it was a dark artifact, made from the subjugation of a higher being. There were other reasons why he might have cautioned them against using it, of course. Blackmailing people was like playing with fire. Done inelegantly, it could easily get out of the extortionist's control and burn their own house down. And if the camera had belonged to a wartime clandestine operation, there might be a whole different caliber of powerful people looking for it.

Samir was old enough to understand the fate awaiting his family if he couldn't provide, yet young enough to be ignorant, reckless, and short-sighted about how to prevent it. He had a magical device in his possession with the staggering potential to turn the tables of their rotten luck. Imagining it from his perspective, it was easy to see why he had thought it a reasonable gamble. It wasn't like it was a gun or anything; it was a *camera*, for God's sake. What real harm could it do?

And, at the end of the day, the final question was this: who wouldn't use every tool in their possession to keep what remained of their family together?

The thought stirred a deep, biting pain in Bernie, and she swallowed hard.

"I understand your position, really, I do," she managed to say around the hard lump in her throat, "but this has to stop. I will take your case to the Order. I'm sure we can find a better solution to your situation."

Now Samir went from sullen to hostile.

"Oh, yes, I'm sure! By forcing Fatima into your ranks, making her fight your battles out on the street, ruining her for—"

"Say one more word," Fatima hissed, eyes narrowed to dangerous slits. "You brought this on all of us with your poor decisions. Don't slap away the charity of the one person that doesn't want to walk over our dead bodies to reach that cursed camera!"

"And it doesn't work like that anyway," Bernie said, as much to Samir as Fatima. "We don't conscript women against their will, and even among those who do join, knighthood is only one path of many. Whether that is of interest to Fatima or not, the Order would help your family regardless. Now: where is the camera?"

Samir's jaw tightened, apparently unconvinced by Bernie's reassurances, stubborn pride and fear wrestling for supremacy inside his rebellious teenage heart.

Then several things happened all at once.

One of the younger boys, Gamal, decided to take the initiative and declare, "I know where the camera is!"

Samir's eyes locked with Bernie's, and they burned with determination as he said, "I saw what's in your photograph."

And Tino swore, "Fuck! We've got company!" as he swiveled away from the window and strode toward the front door, his dress shoes loud on the wooden floorboards.

All the blood drained from Bernie's face, and she stood frozen despite the urgency in Tino's voice.

"Company?" Fatima cried, instantly snatching her pan up again and adjusting the child on her hip. "Who?"

"Some muscle from the Genna brothers' outfit. Musta seen us or heard somethin', or one of your neighbors tattled. They'll be up here in no time."

A swirl of action tore through the small kitchen as Fatima marshaled her younger siblings and Tino paced before the front door like an angry tiger in a cage. But Bernie and Samir remained motionless in the center, eyes boring into each other's.

Bernie's thoughts kept turning in on themselves, focusing down to one salient fact:

Samir had seen the negative.

Her breath caught in her lungs as her throat closed. The air became dense, crushing, and all the warmth fled her bones.

He knew.

Oh God, *he knew!*

CHAPTER SIX

"BERNIE!"

Her name finally cut through the revelation freezing her in place. Tino was watching the front door, grim. "You need me for somethin', or should I just see myself out?"

There wasn't much he could do. Like he'd told the practitioners outside The Blackstone, he couldn't do much to normal people. He was preternaturally strong and resilient; there were practically no scenarios in which a non-practicing human could harm him, while practically every scenario in which he fought back ended in maiming, death, and public backlash. By the Order's own laws, he couldn't engage in physical altercations with non-practitioners. Doing so risked the Order's very serious, very unforgiving wrath, even in those hypothetical cases where his actions were in defense of others. The risk to the larger practicing community if there was a public outcry would be too great.

She'd have to handle them herself, then. She forced herself

back into the present.

"Get them out," she told Tino. Meeting Fatima's eyes, she added, "Go to Order Headquarters and wait for me there." Then, to Tino again, "Don't let *him* out of your sight." She gestured at Samir.

Orders given, she prepared herself, only half-listening as Tino herded the family toward the fire escape, issuing a few sharp commands of his own along the way, colorfully enhanced by liberal use of swear words. With surprising alacrity they had slipped out the window, Fatima's figure at the rear disappearing just as the thud of footsteps became audible in the corridor beyond the front door.

A calm descended over Bernie, bringing with it a liberating kind of focus. She unclasped the scabbarded sword from her baldric, felt the steel's heft in her hand, and approached the door.

She reached it just as a knock sounded.

"Yes?" she called.

"Miss Al-Katib? We're from building management. Would you mind opening up?"

Through the peephole in the door, she glimpsed three men, dark-haired and olive-complected, wearing simple but clean suits. They looked respectable. Perhaps they were, when they weren't doing dirty deeds for the Genna brothers.

Time to test how much the Terrible Gennas respected the Order.

"This is Knight-Maiden Chandler of the Chicago Order of Joan," she announced through the door. "The Al-Katib family is now under Order protection. If you have business with them, I advise taking it up with their Order-assigned representative."

Grimaces and murmurs were exchanged between them.

"Ain't *you* an Order representative?"

She smiled slightly from her side of the door.

"I suppose so."

"Well we'll direct our question to you then: where's the camera?"

She might have said, "That's none of your concern," or "I have no idea what you're talking about." But there was a song singing in her blood now, fear and anger and anguish distilling in her veins to become something new; a vicious, vital thing that rejected the weight crushing her every waking moment of every day. A negative of herself that wanted to scream and rage and burn away the heaviness smothering her, and anything else that happened to get in her way.

So, before she thought better of it, she sighed, "Oh, I imagine it's around here somewhere."

Upon witnessing the immediate, galling effect her words had on the three mafiosos, Bernie twisted to the side and waited, shifting her grip on the sheathed sword in anticipation.

It didn't take long for them to make their move. The front door shuddered under the first kick, flew open on the second. The first man started through, his pistol drawn. He didn't make it over the threshold upright. With expert precision, Bernie swung the sword and struck him dead in the center of his forehead with its pommel. He stumbled and dropped to the floor with a groan, barely catching himself before he slammed his chin against the polished wood, the gun flying from his hand and sliding under the sitting room's coffee table.

The second almost tripped over the first, granting Bernie an easy opportunity to seize his gun-slinging arm and lock it at the elbow between her arm and the unyielding length of steel in her other hand. He yelped as she whirled them around to face the third man, already leveling his pistol at her. She aimed the grappled man's arm and applied a little extra pressure to the elbow lock. He cried out again, his hand involuntarily tensing, and a shot split the air. Blood sprayed from the third man's foot, and he howled, toppling over.

"Bitch!" the second man snarled, and tried to break free. With another judicious application of pressure, she broke his arm. His grunts of discomfort transformed into a scream, and the gun fell from his hand. She kicked it away.

The third man still had his heater, though. Another shot sounded, harsh and close. The bullet blasted past her, missing her only by a few inches. She did not appreciate being shot at. Finally releasing the second man, she shoved him roughly toward the third. They tumbled down together, tangled up in a confusion of broken and bleeding appendages. Another pommel-strike to the third man's wrist saw the last gun fumbled. Then it was just her and the three men rolling around on the ground, moaning and panting, struggling to find it in themselves to get up—a scenario that under different, less bloody circumstances could have been the ingredients for a marvelously entertaining evening.

Behind her, she heard a noise. She twisted, instantly alert, her sword held up to bludgeon any new assailants.

What she saw instead was Samir making his way back toward the fire escape, the camera clutched close to his chest. Bernie blinked, stunned. He'd come back for it! He'd left his sisters and brothers behind and waded through a fight, bullets flying, to get it!

He was halfway through the window already when he froze, eyes fixed further down the fire escape.

"Get back here!" she heard Tino bellow up at him, right before Samir turned to scramble up the fire escape instead of down and she was borne to the floor.

The breath gusted out of her. Hands grabbed her and flipped her over, and she found herself staring up into a face flushed red with anger and sweaty with pain. The third man, she registered. He'd plucked up enough gumption to try for round two.

He shouted an obscenity at her, teeth flashing, spit flying. His meaty hands pinned her upper arms to the ground, his crushing weight on top of her chest. But the Order trained them to handle scenarios such as this. She thrust her hips up, bucking his weight partially off her, then threw her legs up and caught him around the neck. With the full power of her lower body, she wrenched him off, flipping up as she pressed him down to the floor and squeezed with her thighs, cutting off his brain's blood supply. His face turned purple beneath her, his hands scrabbling at her thighs to pry them apart, fingers catching on her silk stockings and leaving red rakes across her sepia skin. But her hold was too strong for him to break, and her adrenaline too high for her to feel any pain, and he passed out within seconds.

Once she knew he was unconscious, she scrambled off him.

Reclaiming her sword, she left the two other men still nursing their wounds and lurched toward the window. She had to get to Samir. She had to get that camera. It wouldn't be long before more goons showed up, not with the commotion they were making.

She had to put an end to all this.

The fire escape's metal struts rattled as she clambered up one short flight. Tino was already there on the rooftop, his back to Bernie. And, she saw, her blood running cold, he'd backed Samir all the way up to the ledge. There was a look of abject terror on the young man's face, and he wobbled precariously on the precipice.

"You got no fuckin' clue the kind of people you're fuckin' with, kid," Tino was saying, his voice deadly calm. "Give me that camera now, or I swear to God, I'll take it off your broken body three stories down."

"Tino, stop!" Bernie shouted. The two men startled. Samir almost slipped. Tino turned toward Bernie, dark glasses no longer hiding his eyes. They shone with resentment at the interruption.

"Bernie," he said, as if he only just remembered she was there, as if he hadn't just been threatening to—what? Intimidate, maybe even push an adolescent boy off a roof? "How nice of you to finally join us." He gestured at Samir. "Maybe you can convince the little twerp to fork it over."

"I can't!" Samir cried. The first tears streaked down his cheeks as he looked between her and Tino. "Don't you see? It's part of our family's heritage, its power our inheritance! How can

I let that slip through our fingers? How can I let go of everything it has to offer, the ability to realize our dreams?" His voice broke when he said, "How can I let our Baba's most guarded secret fall into the hands of strangers?"

Silently, Bernie gestured for Tino to back up. He did, slowly, looking like he regretted every step that took him further away from his goal, whatever that might be. Surely he hadn't decided to take the camera for himself at this late stage, not when the Order would know of his participation in these events? Even if he silenced Bernie, dozens of people had seen them together.

Whatever his angle, he wouldn't have a chance to play it out. Not now that Bernie had taken control of the situation again.

"Samir," Bernie began, carefully lowering her sword to the ground and holding out her empty hands, "I'm sorry this happened to your family. I'm sorry you lost your father, and your mother before him. I know how devastating that is, and how much you want to hold onto anything that meant something to him. But your father's most guarded secret isn't a secret any longer. You can't build the life you wanted with it now, and you can't protect it any more. But you don't need to. You can let it go."

The young man, looking very much now like a frightened boy, had taken a couple steps forward and was no longer a finger's breadth from disaster. The wind was cold, and he shook with it, not having had time to grab a coat before fleeing their apartment. As Bernie's speech came to a close, he hugged the camera tighter, his black hair whipping around his face as he turned pleading eyes on her.

"This camera is our father's greatest work! What son would I be to give it away?"

A memory fluttered up from some distant archive deep in Bernie's brain. Recalling it, her throat tightened. She repeated words once said to her by her father, words she'd forgotten, or didn't believe anymore, but seemed right for Samir and this moment.

"That camera is not your father's greatest work. You are. You and your brothers and sisters. *You* are his legacy. And you would be a good son and a good brother to let it go." She fought to keep her voice steady, struggling to swallow before adding, "Trust me when I tell you that power like what's in that camera is heavy, and it gets heavier every day. If you have the opportunity to leave it behind, leave it and never look back."

The wind roared in her ears as she waited, watching, hoping the boy before her would hear her honesty, her pain, and listen to reason.

Shivering, he looked down at the camera. It was such a simple contraption, completely innocuous, a brown box with one hole like a single shiny black eye and a silver lever and twist key on the adjacent side. It did not look like an object of unspeakable value, powered by a being of frightening potential. It did not look like something people would kill and die for, or a prison of unusual proportions, one that trapped its djinni and holder alike; the djinni with unseen magics, and the photographer with promises of wealth and power, then fear and paranoia.

Leave it, she willed him, *and never look back.*

Samir released a harsh breath, almost a sob, that the wind

snatched away as soon as it left his mouth. He clutched it closer for a moment—then held it out to Bernie.

Scarcely daring to breathe, she took it. The leather case was cold against her fingertips, the little black eye pointing up at her. Only once it was firmly in her grip did she sigh, the warmth of relief flowing down her limbs and loosening them.

"Come on," she said, flashing Samir a sympathetic smile, "let's get you somewhere warm."

"Not so fast!"

The voice struck Bernie's back like a blow. The tension returned, her heart swooping in her chest. She turned, seeking the newest complication to this whole cursed situation.

It was the first mobster she'd laid out, the one she'd struck in the forehead. An ugly purple goose egg rose above his eyebrows, and he stumbled a bit as he finished climbing the fire escape and stepped onto the rooftop. He wouldn't have presented much of a problem if he hadn't retrieved his gun from the floorboards downstairs. Now he held it leveled at them, hammer cocked. It wobbled a bit, but not so much that he couldn't plug a hole in one of them if he squeezed off a couple shots. And he was standing between them and the best exit off the rooftop. She didn't like the other option.

Samir raised his hands. Bernie froze, the camera held close to her chest. Tino barely twitched. He met Bernie's eye and lifted one shoulder in the smallest shrug, almost as if to say, *What do you want* me *to do about it?*

"Hand it over," the man demanded, stepping closer, his balance more sure on the flat surface. "Now!"

Bernie firmed her stance. "No."

His mouth bent into a snarl.

"I'll blow your fuckin' head off, you little bitch, I swear to God! You and every other bull-dagger with a sword are gonna hear from the Gennas, mark my words! Now put it on the ground and slide it over! And you! Turn around and let me see 'em, old man!"

That caught Tino's attention.

"Old man?" He turned to face the mafioso, and the other man's face drained of all color, making the knob on his forehead all the uglier. "Don't see any of those around here. Dead ones, though, now that's another story."

"Morandi," the mobster whispered, his free hand instantly flying up to cross himself.

Tino took a casual step toward him.

"You're not gonna get that camera."

The man wrapped his second hand around the pistol grip, stabilizing it.

"Don't come no closer, I-I mean it!"

"Do you?" Tino took another step. He sounded bored. "Do you really?"

Sweat beaded on the man's forehead, his eyes wide with fear as Tino closed by another step.

He twitched the gun over to Bernie again.

"Not another step forward, or she gets it!"

Tino paused. In her chest, Bernie's heart thudded hard against her ribcage. There was no love lost between her and Tino. He'd seemed to like Dot, and look where that'd gotten her! The Order wouldn't be pleased by Bernie's death, but then he could argue that they'd told him not to get involved with mundies under any circumstance. If she was a casualty of that rule, then so be it.

She was sure the same calculations were running through Tino's head from where he stood a few feet ahead of her.

"That's right," the mobster crowed. "Stay right there or you'll be pickin' up little red chunks of your new knight-whore off the shingles."

At that, the demi straightened from his insouciant posture. Something in the atmosphere shifted, drew taut, snatched the air from Bernie's lungs.

Tino took one deliberate step sideways, blocking Bernie's view of the mobster.

"You been to confession lately?" he asked, his voice a low rumble.

Bernie shifted slightly, just enough that she could see a sliver of the man's face over Tino's broad shoulder. Whatever he saw in Tino's face, his own had gone slack with horror.

"Because," Tino went on, resuming his slow, rolling trek toward the gunman, "you pull that trigger, I'll put you on the express train to Hell before you can say 'Requiescat in pace.'"

The gun twitched up from Tino's stomach to his head.

"S-stop, or th-this one goes between your fucked-up devil eyes," he stammered.

The wind carried Tino's soft, mirthless laugh to Bernie.

"Do it," he said. It sounded like he was smiling. "See what happens."

What the hell was he doing? Did he think the mobster was bluffing? Did he think that he could survive a bullet right to the brain pan? Sure, she'd heard demies were capable of surviving otherwise mortal injuries, but they were rare creatures, with fewer than ten known cases listed in the Archives and only half of those were first-hand accounts. The Order was old; guns, particularly the kinds now available on the streets, were new.

If that guy blasted Tino between the eyes, Bernie wasn't sure he'd survive. Even if he did, he certainly wouldn't be in any condition to help her.

And why wasn't Tino just disarming him? Demies were fast, almost as fast as vampires. He should be able to do it.

Because he wanted to tempt fate, she realized. He wanted whatever came next. Whether that was death or carnage, she wasn't sure, but she sure as hell wasn't going to find out.

The camera in her hands was the problem. It was an abomination, created to plunder people's secrets, expose their lives and destroy them. She wasn't going to let it fall into the clutches of the gangs or the covens, who would use it for their own ends. But, in a flash of insight that struck like lightning and left her burning with its revelation, neither could she give it to the Order. Because the truth was, this thing shouldn't exist. The Order might put it away, but the temptation would always be there: what if they could use it, but for good? What if they could target criminals, get the evidence they needed to put dangerous people away? Then, despite their better judgment, the reasoning might shift to: what if they could use it to silence another new category of dangerous people? The Order had enemies, many people and organizations who would like nothing more than to see them fail, many of which tried all they could to bring such an end about. Why not use it against them to protect the Order? Why not use it for the greater good?

The Order kept many dangerous objects, locked away in deep vaults never to be used. Throughout their history, they'd successfully contained threat after threat while resisting the siren song of their power. But it only took a few less-than-scrupulous leaders to jeopardize that, and it would be so easy to justify bending the rules for this camera. After all, just as she was sure Samir had reasoned, it wasn't like it could kill people.

At the end of the day, no one should have that power.

And, perhaps most salient of all, at the heart of that power was a being's pain.

So Bernie made a decision.

She raised the camera over her head and hurled it down with all her strength.

CHAPTER SEVEN

THERE WAS a splintering crack and the bright sound of shattering glass as the camera opened up and spilled its insides across the rooftop. And then—

Then a wave washed over her, blowing back the October cold with a blizzard of pinprick needles across her skin. A murder of crows, startled from their perch in the nearby skeletal tree, froze mid-flight, as did the shards of glass from the camera's broken lens. As did everything else around Bernie, except for Tino.

He was twisting toward her, slow as molasses, his mouth parting and eyes wide. Only, it didn't seem that *he* was moving, exactly, as much as the demon inside him, a lurid golden double dragging him around to face her. In that moment, he looked like a double-exposure, one shining body superimposed over the other, the ephemeral pulling the solid behind it. In this form he seemed to have three eyes: one of pure, searing light, entirely inhuman; one wide and brown, expressive as any man's; and the one where the infernal and mundane overlapped, the eye she recognized as his, a glowing golden ring around a cold black center.

And, rising from inside the broken camera between her and Tino, was the freed djinni.

It moved like a heat shimmer over desert sand or summer asphalt. When it spoke, it did so without sound, the words instead rippling through her and reverberating around her mind, thunderously loud.

Ahhh, it boomed, *free at last! Free to return to my homeland, my people! Free to pursue my vengeance on the one who dared trap me! A price must be paid, and there is blood yet to pay it.*

With a horrible lurch, Bernie understood the djinni's meaning. Samir and his family.

"But you can't!" she exclaimed. Then, feeling the weight of the djinni's disapproval and growing wrath on her, she searched for a way to dissuade it. "The sins of one man are his own and belong to him alone. His father imprisoned you, not him!"

And yet the boy knew I was the heart of his torturous machine, and he used me anyway. That sin is his own, and it caused me great pain.

"Even so," Bernie reasoned, her voice warbling on the words. "It is forbidden by Allah to take the life of another."

Allah! the djinni raged, and a blast of heat smacked Bernie's face and snatched at her clothes, hot as the breath of a furnace. *Think you that I am His creature? I do not answer to His authority, and I never shall!* The temperature dropped suddenly to something more comfortable. Bernie blinked, her eyes parched of moisture in the wake of its outburst.

But you have done me a great boon, and so, as is right, I will offer you a great boon in return. Ask for what you desire, and if it is within my power to give, it shall be yours. And my power is great indeed.

Anything she desired? A fountain of longing welled up and burst free, and suddenly she was nothing but a being of longing, wanting, needing.

She could make so much right with a single sentence, restore so much that she had lost, regain pieces of herself she long thought gone forever.

Still, she hesitated before she asked, "Can you bring back the dead?"

The djinni shifted, its slender, ephemeral body stretching up like a flame given more fuel.

…It is within my power, it said, its words a subdued rumble in her chest.

"Can you bring back only one person, or many?"

The djinni considered it. *Many is within my power. The number which you hold in your hand is my limit.*

The waters within her rose, threatening to pull her into their undertow. She gasped, the pain in her chest sharp, and tried to steady herself. Then it was possible? Could she really have her heart's greatest desire?

Dizzily, she asked, "Would they be as they were? Would there be consequences?"

There are always consequences, human. I am powerful, but I am not of such an order that I could raise them whole and new, as complete as they once were. They would be diminished, but alive they would be. They would speak, and feel, and apprehend their surroundings. They would not be the same, but they would be by your side again, for good or for ill.

The hope buoying her up sagged, her heart dropping precipitously in her chest. They wouldn't be the same. Of course they wouldn't be. But… wouldn't it be worth it, to have them here with her again? For good or for ill, the djinni said, like a bad tiding. But how was that any different from life and all its ups and downs?

She tried to convince herself that it would be no different, but in her heart of hearts, she knew that wasn't true.

Well, maybe not *them*, then, but what if she brought just one person back? What if she could erase the pain of her latest loss?

Behind the djinni, Tino and his demon were still moving. He was finishing his turn toward her, one hand rising, his mouth opening to form a word. She met his eyes, looked into them. She couldn't begin to guess what the demon was feeling. The demi's gold-ringed eye was just as inscrutable as ever. But his human eye… The black at its center was a pit of longing as voracious as hers, and inside was a spark of something else. Desperation, she thought, though she couldn't be sure. It was shaded by a yawning need which knew no end, swallowed by its depths.

She could do it. With one word, one name, she could speak a human back into being. Dot, her friend, her mentor, in many ways her savior. She could right the wrong of her death, let go of the guilt and grief. Watch Tino face the woman he'd failed, the woman he'd left to the wolves, her life thrown away as carelessly as a spent cigarette. What a sight that would be!

She could have at least one thing back.

But it wouldn't be real. The djinni had said as much. Whatever came back might look like Dot, but it would lack something essential. It wouldn't be fair to Dot, and Bernie was not so far gone that she would settle for less than the whole of her friend. She wanted truth, not pretty illusions. She wanted it all or nothing.

As those wishes, her most dear desires, died, another came to take its place. If she couldn't have them, maybe she could free herself from—

That I cannot do, the djinni stated, and it was like hurtling into a brick wall. *Nor could any power I know short of the one I reject so adamantly.*

She pressed her face into her hands, the loss of it all crashing over her again. The world in her hands, and yet everything she desired transcended even that, reaching into powers beyond reason or imagination.

Yet a wish she still had.

Taking a deep breath, she searched for a new one, and found it.

"The person you intend to extract your vengeance from is barely more than a child, as are the remaining members of his family." She looked up at the djinni, felt the tears on her cheeks dry to salt before its heat. "This is the boon you will grant me: you will strike the memory of this boy and his family from the minds of any who would wish to harm him, including yourself, if need be."

The djinni flared, its shape widening in a ripple of shock. Then it pulled tight again, becoming long and impossibly tall, like the water spout she'd seen on Lake Michigan once.

The boon is given, the deed done. I am free at last. Farewell, chosen of the powers!

In a flash as bright as lightning, it disappeared, and the world burst into motion again.

The mobster swayed on his feet, his grip slacking to let the pistol fall onto the hard rooftop. Behind her, Samir sucked in a deep, needy breath, his shoe soles scuffing as he presumably tried to stay upright.

In front of her, Tino stumbled forward. When his eyes met hers, both pupils were once again rimmed with gold, the only visible trace of his infernal double now safely locked away again under his skin. They were wide, their focus on her singularly intense.

"What the fuck did you just do?" he demanded.

She brushed the salt from her skin and sniffed. The October cold had returned, deeper than before.

"I'd hoped you hadn't heard." Once again, his demi nature had fouled up the works.

"Anything!" he hissed, striding toward her. "Isn't that what it said? You coulda had *anything*, and you threw it away on that worthless, waste-of-space runt? What the fuck is wrong with you?"

Of course he wouldn't understand, rich cat that he was, what it was like to live one failed paycheck away from destitution.

Of course he wouldn't understand, part-demon that he was, the value of a stranger's life.

He stopped short before he reached her, and she saw it clearly: a madness, near hysteria, capering behind his glowing eyes. But now he wasn't looking at her. He stared past her, into whatever future he imagined he could have had. His breath came fast as he pressed a hand to his forehead, fingers threading through his bone-white locks, finally laying waste to what remained of his carefully styled coiffure.

"I coulda—with that wish, I coulda—!"

"You could have what?" Bernie shot back. "What would you have wished for, Tino? More money? Power? Women?"

Her words had an instant, calcifying effect on him. Despite the light perpetually ringing his eyes, they darkened. The strange agitation disappeared from them, replaced by a cold-blooded remoteness as he looked back at her, statue-still.

"No, I don't need more women in my life," he said, his tone as sharp as a razor and as dead as its steel. "Just one less."

"Don't you mean *another* less?" Bernie retorted.

His nostrils flared and his jaw clenched for a fraction of a second. He passed a look over her, detached, dismissive, and utterly contemptuous. Then, slow and easy, a hostile smile lit his face and the fire in his eyes burned hot again. Hotter than before, even. There was an especially hellish quality to them, a fire in them that blazed with hateful scorn. He huffed a short, dry laugh and inclined his head in a mockery of good manners.

"See ya around, Bernie," he said, and walked away, stepping around the clearly confused mobster and descending the fire escape. Dazed, the mafioso followed after him, leaving his gun on the rooftop behind him.

Bernie sighed and sagged, hugging herself against the October cold. Anything. That's what Tino said she could have had. But he was wrong. She could have had anything except her heart's desire. And right now, that felt a lot like nothing at all.

"Thank you," a watery voice said from just over her shoulder. Samir was hovering there, looking younger still and quite lost.

She tried to smile. "I bought you a second chance. Thank me by doing some good with it."

He looked out across the city, wracking his brain for what that good might be.

"I'd say taking care of your family is about as great a good as a person can do. Letting yourself be happy whenever the occasion arises and wherever you can claim it is a close second. Just try not to confuse things that offer you brief pleasure with things that make you happy." She paused before adding, "And I think we can safely rule blackmail schemes out of the 'good' column."

He nodded. The wind gusted over them as he stood, still looking out at the city, his mouth twisting as he turned over that thought. Bernie waited beside him feeling numb inside and out.

Samir opened his mouth, hesitated, then carried on.

"I didn't see your secret," he confessed, his words almost snatched away by the wind. "I didn't want to give the camera up, so I lied. I'm sorry."

Bernie closed her eyes, the heavy weight lightening in her chest. Her heart performed one painful flip from the unexpected shift.

"Whatever it was, Knight Chandler, I'm sure Allah forgives you."

That wasn't true. What she'd done felt like it could never be forgiven. If it could be, He wouldn't have cursed her with the burden she bore.

It was a nice sentiment, though.

"You're freezing," she said. "Go grab your coat and warm up. It should be safe for you now. When you're thawed out, head to Order Headquarters. I'll meet you there when I've cleaned things up here."

Beside her, Samir nodded. Then, moving quickly, he folded his arms around her in a brief but oh-so-tight hug.

"Thank you," he breathed into her ear, then released her and hurried down the fire escape, leaving Bernie alone on the rooftop, letting the wind scrape away the last traces of her tears.

CHAPTER EIGHT

THERE HADN'T just been any mountain of paperwork waiting for her. It was the Mount Everest of paperwork, in addition to all three Knight-Matrons and the Marshal of the Chicago Order, all demanding answers for how a simple investigate-and-confiscate had turned into a fiasco that caused twelve injuries requiring hospitalization (several of the practitioners from The Blackstone alley, all three of the mafiosos Bernie had fought, plus another Fatima had laid out with her frying pan on their way down the fire escape), sixteen (thankfully minor) automobile accidents, one fire, a flurry of alternating demands and profuse apologies from covens and criminal organizations alike, hundreds of dollars in damages on top of the $2,500 pledged to the Temperance League, and finally, a petition from a family of five orphans for Order protection and assistance.

What had been a long day became a very, very long night.

It was dawn before she was dismissed to go home and get some rest. But, in a queer turn of events, she was so tired she couldn't go to sleep. She supposed that was just fine; she still had work to do.

She'd stashed the stacks of photographs back at her apartment. Her roommate, Lula, had gone home to Wisconsin for a week to help care for her ailing mother, which meant Bernie could bring as many men back to their room as she could sneak past the proprietress. Unfortunately, so far that number had been depressingly small at only two, and now she had an apartment full of what might technically qualify as illegally obtained evidence to burn.

She didn't think of it as evidence, exactly. These secrets had been stolen and sealed in photographic form illicitly in the first place. Whether they exposed crimes, guilty pleasures, or just plain guilt was none of her or anybody else's business.

She packed them into an old, worn-out suitcase and took a trip to the lakeshore. This late in the year, the jungle campsite behind the Field Museum that Chicago's thriving hobo population favored would be emptier, many members of its transient population seeking out warmer accommodations for the winter months, but there would still be a few around. When she arrived, she found two men huddled up next to a trash can fire, their faces close together, their grins illuminated by its warm glow as dainty snowflakes began to fall over the city.

She greeted them, chatted for a minute, then paid them for the use of their fire and some privacy. Handful by handful, she shoveled the photographs into the flames, watched their glossy edges curl and their faces and ghostly apparitions bubble up and blister away. Toward the bottom of the suitcase, she caught sight of Tino's face among those in the next offering. He looked out at her, his unnatural eyes calm and expectant. She teased his photograph free and tossed the rest in the can, listening to them crackle and hiss as she examined his captured likeness again.

Nothing had changed about the photograph. No secrets dogged the demi, no phantoms floated tauntingly around him, just out of reach. She was sure he had many nasty ones; their absence did not indicate innocence, simply that the demi's inherently magic-warping nature had saved him again.

It was profoundly unfair, how something as unholy as him could move through life without any of its muck sticking to him. He stared up at her, wooden and unfeeling. She wondered if he had looked like that when he'd heard the news about Dot.

Why wonder? Of course he had.

Demies were all humans once, or so the Order's texts claimed, before they transformed somehow into a strange confluence of mortal and infernal. Was there any humanity left in him, any at all?

She thought there might be, in some small measure. She'd seen it there on the rooftop, in that strange liminal space the djinni created when the demon inside Tino had briefly slipped out of register with the rest of him. There might have been something there in the brown of his eye, some memory of what it was like to feel… Well, something human.

Whatever flicker might have been there, it was gone when he'd returned to normal. Only a vast distance looked back at her, the same smug remoteness Tino had always exhibited in anything he did.

And his parting words, spoken so venomously:

See ya around, Bernie.

They had been a threat, she was sure. Not that he could act on it. Not without the Order ensuring that was the last thing he ever did. She was sure he liked living too much to pursue any grudge he might hold against her.

See ya around, Bernie.

Yeah, not if she could help it.

With that thought, she fed his photo to the fire and watched as the monster on its face was reduced to ash in a way he never could be in real life.

She emptied the suitcase before reaching into her black overcoat's pocket and tossing in two of the three strips of negatives. The last… she wasn't quite ready to dispose of yet. She didn't want to do it here, anyway. It felt too exposed.

There was one last stop she needed to make before she could return home and destroy the final secrets captured by the djinni camera. She didn't bother taking the suitcase. It wasn't monogrammed, and she'd already promised it to the transient couple along with a dollar to sweeten the deal and ensure their silence. Her hands were free when she left the park, and she filled them again with flowers bought from a stand on the way to the cemetery.

Dot's grave was at the crest of a hill. The marker was nicer than most; she hadn't had any family to speak of, at least not any willing to claim her, and the Order had footed her burial bill. Like all knights killed in the line of duty, she was laid to rest under a granite marker carved with the Order's seal. Underneath was her name, Dorothy Jenkins, her birth date and death date, and the simple but devastatingly true epitaph: She lived boldly and died bravely.

The dying grass, now dusted with snow, crunched under Bernie's winter boots. There was less grass covering her grave, having barely had enough time to grow over the disturbed earth before the first hard frost had halted its progress. There was already an urn of flowers placed next to her headstone, their stalks withered and dry, the blossoms carried away by the past month's blustery winds. The overflowing arrangements that had covered her grave site at her funeral two months prior had long since been cleared away.

Bernie knelt, tenderly setting her bunch of yellow, late-season chrysanthemums against Dot's marker. They stood out bright and colorful against the snow and gray stone.

"Sorry I'm late," she said. "But I think you should forgive me, considering all the times I forgave you for showing up hours after you should have."

The headstone sat quietly at her feet, unable to answer.

Bernie sighed, her breath billowing out in front of her.

"Yes, I'm late even by your standards, I know. If you have such a problem with that, you can climb right out of your coffin and tell me all about it."

Nothing stirred under her feet. Bernie, of course, hadn't expected anything like that to happen, not really, and if something had… Well, she was a knight. It was her job to put a stop to nonsense like that.

Dot would understand.

The thought brought an abrupt surge of tears into her eyes.

She'd failed her. She didn't know how, but she felt it deep in her bones. She'd wronged Dot somehow. By becoming her friend, by relying on that friendship, Bernie had condemned her.

And now she was dead.

"I miss you," she whispered. It felt like a scream. It echoed around in the empty places inside her, howling, fathomless. And then she was sobbing, her hand clasped against her mouth, trying to hold it all in. Little flakes of snow caught on her eyelashes, stuck to her cheeks and melted into her tears.

The grave gave no answer and offered no comfort. It remained, fixed and heavy and—no matter how hard Bernie wished it to be otherwise—inarguably real.

She heard steps behind her, growing louder. The cold air hurt her lungs as she sucked in breath after breath, trying to steady herself. She only just managed to gain control of her breathing when one of the groundskeepers appeared at her side. Bernie turned her face away, not trusting herself to speak.

There was a dry rustling and a grunt as the groundskeeper set something down. His footsteps retreated. When Bernie looked back at the headstone, the dead flowers in the urn had been replaced by fresh ones.

It was a beautiful arrangement, full of white and pale blue flowers, lilies and columbines and sprays of baby's breath and other flowers both out-of-season and exotic. The urn itself, Bernie finally noticed, was of finely worked white jade. It was, quite obviously, exorbitantly expensive, as were the flowers it held.

A card fluttered on the silk ribbon holding the bouquet together. Bernie stooped to catch it between her gloved fingers.

It read: *I was wrong. I do miss you.*

"Excuse me!" Bernie shouted, turning to see the groundskeeper slowly making his way through the headstones with a wheelbarrow full of bouquets. He halted as she jogged toward him, careful not to tread on any of the graves.

"Yes?" he said, voice muffled beneath the scarf wrapped around his nose and mouth.

"Who sent those flowers to Miss Jenkins?" she asked.

The groundskeeper's eyebrows drew together. He pushed his flat cap back from his silver-streaked, tightly coiled hair and scratched his forehead thoughtfully.

"Well, miss, I can't really say—"

"Oh please," Bernie pleaded, her throat tight with the threat of more tears, "I must know."

The undertaker paused and laid a flat look on her.

"If you'd let me finish, I was gonna say because I don't know. Their donor is anonymous. Gal musta meant something to them, though, because they bought a fresh bouquet for her every month for the next ten years."

Bernie bit her lip, thinking.

"Need anything else, miss?"

She shook her head. "Oh, no. Thank you, sir."

Bernie returned to Dot's grave and its flowers, both hers and the ones in the jade urn. She stared at them a long time, entertaining all the possibilities for who could afford such an extravagance, and who would care enough to shell out for it.

Dot had had a lot of lovers from all walks of life. They used to joke she'd broken hearts from every tax bracket the IRS defined.

Even then, her mind kept producing the same answer, however improbable.

No, not improbable. Impossible. It must be someone else. She was only thinking of Tino because of everything that had just happened. He wouldn't waste a nickel on a Joan, not even Dot now that she was dead. The most he might muster would be the water to spit on her grave, if he ever paid it a visit.

I was wrong. I do miss you.

Bernie carried those words inside her as she made her way back to her apartment and closed the door behind her, sealing the outer world away.

It was dim inside, the furniture lit by only the pale light reflecting off the snowfall coming through their modest windows. She left the lights off and made her way to their cramped kitchen and its fold-down linoleum table.

Fingers shaking, she pulled her gloves off and stuck one hand inside her coat pocket.

The film was slick in her fingers as she pulled it out. She knew her image had to be on this strand because it hadn't been on the other two, but she hadn't looked at it yet. She was scared to. There were many secrets it might show, all of which she'd tried to forget. She'd half-convinced herself they were nightmares, or perhaps the unreliable memories of a troubled child.

Whatever the case, she'd tried to leave it all behind her. She still hoped it would stay back there, in the graveyard of her childhood.

Slowly, she held the film up to the white square of the window and scanned it.

Black box after black box passed between her fingers. A man, a woman, three laughing faces in one frame. Cold sweat beaded on her forehead, her fingers turned clammy. More people, none of them her. She was almost to the end of the roll. Maybe he'd run out of film before—

And then she found herself, black netella draped over her cropped curls, her eyes tired and sad above lips forced into a wry smile. Behind her was a crush of people who might have been laughing and talking, but it was impossible to tell; their figures were blurred and distorted beneath streaks of phantom light. Even in the film they seemed to shimmer and glow faintly, as if the celluloid had physically trapped light between its fibers. Together, they formed a nimbus around her and extended beyond the frame, the bulk of their mass uncaptured by the relatively narrow scope of the camera.

Wings. And they were many.

Bernie stared at it, as frozen in place as her likeness in the picture.

She didn't know how long she stood there, only that the light had dimmed further by the time she managed to make herself move.

She went for the matches in the bottom kitchen drawer. The tremor had left her fingers by the time she struck one, but sensation had yet to return. The small point of flame touched the ribbon's edge; the fire spread quickly, making an easy meal of the celluloid.

Bernie dropped it into the sink and watched it burn away, the damning evidence that her nightmares were real and the past wasn't nearly as dead as she hoped. As the last scrap of film curled away beneath the fire's gnawing teeth, she took comfort in knowing that, for a time at least, her heavy secret was made light as smoke. Safe again.

For now.

ACKNOWLEDGEMENTS

Thank you to all the lovely members of The Lore Writing Club, who were the first to read (and approve!) this fiction. For many, this was their entry point into the Joaniverse, and their enthusiasm proved to me that *Strange Developments* could stand on its own as well as entice readers to seek out more from the Degrees of Magic series and the Joaniverse.

Thank you again to my mother, who has championed our cause and supported us every step of the way. Thank you to James Mitchell Lewis, who yet again worked his magic on this cover (and put up with my hovering all the while). Thank you to my husband, Jamie, who continues to offer his excellent editorial advice while cheering me on night and day, day in and day out. Thank you to all our patrons on *The Harrowing of Minerva Damson*'s Patreon who have continued to support us despite our hiatus. Thank you to CeAnn Lewis for upping our promo game and fangirling all over the place about *First-Degree Magic* and *Strange Developments* alike. Just... loads of thank yous all around to all our family, friends, and fans. Your love and enthusiasm breathes greater life and soul into my art, and for that I am unfathomably grateful.

GLOSSARY OF USEFUL INFORMATION

NETELA

Part of the traditional Ethiopian mode of dress, a netela is a lightweight shawl with embroidered edges that is worn about the head and shoulders. The way it is worn can communicate a variety of information about the wearer such as marital status, religious affiliation, social status, and wealth.

JOLLY RICE

"Jolly rice" is the colloquial A'nowalkówan term for jollof rice, a popular West African dish typically reserved for celebrations and big gatherings. There are myriad ways to make jollof rice—regional variations vie to be the "best" in friendly competition with each other. Jolly rice is a beloved and highly popular dish in A'nowalkówa, as American as apple pie. Additionally, other food traditions have added their own twist to jolly rice, making it distinct from its progenitors. Jolly manoomin, as seen on the

Temperance League's Luncheon Menu, replaces a good portion of the white rice in the traditional recipe with wild rice, called manoomin by the Ojibwe people.

KITFO

An Ethiopian form of beef tartare, kitfo is raw beef marinated in nitter kibbeh (a clarified butter) and spices that is served slightly warmed. A delicacy.

'ILM AL LIMIYA

One of the occult sciences of Islam, this branch of knowledge teaches the subjugation of spirits and other higher beings through mental prowess and spiritual strength.

LADIES TEMPERANCE LEAGUE'S
Autumn Charity Luncheon

THE BLACKSTONE, CHICAGO   OCTOBER, 1925

▪▪▪ MENU ▪▪▪

Mixed Nuts   Cattalo Kitfo Tartare   Deviled Eggs

Spiced Pumpkin Consummé   Sauce d'Arachide

Trout Véronique   Jollof Manoomin

Venison Wellington, Whipped Buttered Parsnips

Beet Greens Gomen   A'nowalkówan Medley   Waldorf Salad

Iced Sumac Punch

Cider-Braised Quail, Wild Mushrooms in Sauce

Sweet Potato Tartlets   Candied Cranberries   Vanilla Ice Cream

Coffee   Chocolat   Tea

Tasting Notes:

<u>Mixed nuts:</u> Toasted. All excellent, particularly the hickory, walnuts, and butternuts.

<u>Cattalo kitfo:</u> I prefer beef to bison—meat from the "cattalo" hybrid sufficed here.

<u>Deviled eggs:</u> Not spicy enough.

<u>Spiced Pumpkin Consummé:</u> Adequate.

<u>Sauce d'Arachide:</u> Peanut soup is decadent as always. This tended to the runnier side. The boiled yams over which it was poured were rustically chopped, if one were to be delicate on the matter.

<u>Trout Veronique:</u> Tansy sauce, flaky fish. A good course.

<u>Jolly manoomin:</u> Delightful, truly. Almost as tasty as our own cook's rendition!

<u>Venison Wellington:</u> Sophisticated and balanced. Not mentioned on the menu: the cranberry sauce accompanying the wellington, which was tangy and bright.

<u>Beet greens somen:</u> Beet greens always taste earthy. My tablemates enjoyed it. I tolerated it.

<u>A'nowalkówan medley:</u> Included amaranth, teff, manoomin, corn, and various beans cooked, chilled, and dressed in a vinaigrette. Refreshing and hearty.

<u>Waldorf salad:</u> As good as the Waldorf Astoria's. Perhaps they hired a chef formerly employed there?

<u>Iced sumac punch:</u> As expected, but perhaps a bit plebian for this event.

<u>Cider-braised quail:</u> A triumph! Stuffed with seasoned, fragrant cornmeal. A delicious morsel!

<u>Wild mushrooms in sauce:</u> Also a revelation. I think I detected a bit of acorn flour in the gravy?

<u>Sweet potato tartlet:</u> Crispy, flaky crust and thick filling just sweet enough. How can I help but love it?

<u>Candied cranberries:</u> The cranberries return for an encore. Adequate.

<u>Vanilla ice cream:</u> Vanilla is always luxurious, naturally, but it cannot compare to the tartlet.

<u>Chocolat:</u> Served the way it should be, bitter and spicy. Bravo!

A worthwhile menu for a worthy event.

A Primer on Preternatural Creatures, Spirits, and the Like for Knights and Squires of the Order of Joan

North American Edition

Boston: 1905

Order of St. Catherine Press

Elementals

All Elementals should be regarded with the greatest respect and caution. ALL ELEMENTALS ARE CREATURES OF FIRST-DEGREE MAGIC. They occupy an ambiguous position in the Divine/Profane paradigm owing to their varied and inconsistent attitudes towards humanity. There are two major theories as to their nature and origin: first, that they are relics of the act of Creation and predate the emergence of Man, regardless of whether we were shaped directly by the hand of God or formed gradually over the course of millennia of evolution; second, that they exist on a plane parallel to our own that is intensely magical in nature. This plane intersects with our own under certain conditions at specific times and places, which would help explain how these creatures can appear and disappear so completely and instantaneously when they desire to do so. There are additional theories, but the above, while divisive, are the most generally accepted among Order scholars.

A Primer on Preternatural Creatures

A significant portion of human knowledge both oral and recorded has been dedicated to informing future generations of the dangers of these beings, how they might be appeased if angered or petitioned if needed, and generally how to interact safely with them—if any safe way exists. Some traditions purport to have discovered means of capturing and controlling Elementals, but these arts are advanced, seldom mastered and seldom used, and always undertaken by exceptionally gifted individuals. Most extant lore focuses on talismans to ward against Elemental attention or gifts that may be offered in exchange for limited services. For much of human history, and indeed in many cultural traditions, there are classes of Elementals that have been known to coexist peacefully alongside humans since time out of memory. Indeed, some are intimately connected to specific places or families, guiding and guarding them, keeping them in good repair or health. Elementals are an incredibly varied class of beings that can help or hinder humans—or ignore them altogether—and thus responses to them are also necessarily varied. They cannot be said to be "good" or "evil," merely different, with agendas that sometimes conflict with our human activities and goals.

In all cases, it is important to remember that Elementals are beings of higher intelligence, even the ones that seem animal or monstrous. While that intelligence may be alien to human reasoning, it is still a kind of logic that is undoubtedly complex and capable. All Elementals should be treated with respect and the same (or greater) courtesy that one might extend to a fellow human being, as they are at least equivalent in intelligence and agency. They are also imminently capable of punishing perceived transgressions with astonishing magical force. Being creatures of high intelligence and possessing a great degree of personal agency, Elementals are liable to take a liking or disliking to humans as capriciously as humans might with each other. Knights should bear this in mind if ever interacting with an Elemental: they can be boon companions or formidable enemies, but never should their allegiances be taken for granted. Whether they are steadfast or fickle in their convictions cannot be known without longer association, and they can change their minds at any time and for reasons that may seem nonsensical to human sensibilities. It is OUR opinion that knights should never undertake association with an Elemental of her own volition without rigorous training. While Elementals are often drawn to humans they judge to be guileless, and while such individuals sometimes are the beneficiaries of great rewards from Elemental-kind, it is a far more precarious position than approaching them, as we would advise, with an informed and clever mind.

As a "class," Elementals are the most varied and complex; even the regionalized selections for this portion of the training materials tend to run extraordinarily long, despite its abbreviated content. Suffice to say that it is impossible to cover the full depth and breadth of Elemental beings here, and that whole careers have been spent pursuing greater understanding of these fantastic beings and beasts. Please bear in mind that the following entries are, by necessity, highly generalized. Most knights go their entire careers without encountering an Elemental. Still, it is best to be prepared for the possibility since the consequences of ignorance are potentially quite punishing.

A Primer on Preternatural Creatures

The following titles particular relevance and interest in regard to elemental topics:

† *Faerie Kinde* by Sister-Superior Annis Goodacre, Order of Joan Exeter Cloister, 1462

† *Known Concordats and Appropriate Concordance with Elfkind* by Magistra Gertrude de Windt, Order of St. Catherine Abbey in Ghent, 1488

† *Right Conduct Toward the Fée* by Knight-Matron Isabeau la Poucelle and the Sisters-Scribes of the Order of Joan Grand Abbey in Paris, 1449

† *A Compendium of the Members of the Tuatha Dé Danann and Aos Sí* by Magistra Aoife Mhig Eilne, Béal Feirste St. Catherine Scriptorium, 1607

† *Sìthe Gifts and Tricks* by Marshal Raghnaid NicRaith, Glasgow Order of Joan, 1626

† *Jötnar Index* by Knight-Matron Gyda Dahlstrøm, Bergen Order of Joan, 1513

† *The World Next to Ours and its Hidden Peoples* by Knight-Courier Nadya Kurilov, Yakutsk Order of Joan, 1898

† *Treatise on the Origin and Nature of Djinn* by Magistra Fajr al-Alami, Tunis Order of St. Catherine Madrassa, 1553

ELEMENTALS

† *The Tribes of Djinn* by Magistra Kahveci Işıl, Ankara Cloister of St. Catherine, 1603

† *The Little Folk of Our Continent* by Sister-Scribe Wanuri Mwangi, Mombasa Order of St. Catherine Grand Scriptorium, 1831

† *Guardians of the Earth* by Magistra Amparo Zúñiga Amayo, Comayagua Order of Joan, 1792

† *Stories of Jogah and Their Like* by Knight-Matron Iontó:rats Tejonihokarawa, Chenango Point Order of Joan, 1847

† *Nvnehi and Yunwi Tsunsdi for Knights Who Must Know* by Sister-Scribe Jola May Pendergrass, Chota Order of Joan, 1856

† *Kachina* by Sister-Scribe Debahayaye Tsisete and Sister-Superior Alasvuhoya Kabotie, Acoma Order of St. Catherine outpost, 1891

† *A List of Kami and Yokai* by Joan no Onna-Musha Hosokawa Chizuko, Kumamoto Order of Joan outpost, 1640, rediscovered and updated by Magistra Uesugi Kiyo, Kyoto Order of Joan, 1887

† *Good and Evil Beings of the Middle Kingdom and Our Neighbors* by Sister-Superior Wei Ruoxi, Beijing Order of Joan, 1761

† *Apsaras and Other Nature Spirits* by Sister-Superior Asha Sharma, Trivandrum Order of Joan, 1792

A Primer on Preternatural Creatures

† *An Argument for the Reclassification of Elementals to Ancient Divinities* by Marshal Makvala Chabukiani, Tbilisi Order of Joan, 1843

† *An Examination of How New Religions Disrupted the Transmission of Vital Knowledge in regards to Ancient Wisdom, Rituals, and Customs Which Harmonized Human Relations with the Supernatural* by Sister-Scribe Zarifa Howayek, Beirut Order of St. Catherine Abbey, 1867

† *Elemental Beasts and Beings* by Knight-Matron Zümrüd Iravani, Baku Order of Joan, 1684

† *The Unicorne, Wyverne, and Other Puissant Creatures of Note* by Feal-Agent Griffith Lloyd, Caerdydd Order of Joan, 1501

† *Myth Made Flesh* by Knight-Maiden Avdotya Suvorova, St. Petersburg Order of Joan, 1712

† *When Belief Becomes Reality: How Man Creates Our Own Gods and Monsters and Collectively Manifest Miracles* by Sister-Superior Karla Moser, Zürich Order of St. Catherine Abbey, 1901

† *Refuting the Assertion that Man Self-Creates Our Reality and All The Beings with which We Share It* by Magistra Sofi Nyland, Gothenburg Order of Joan, 1902

In THE UNITED STATES OF AMERICA, for which this primer has been produced, the following are the likely beings one might encounter. BEAR IN MIND THAT BECAUSE OF THE HIGH CONCENTRATION OF IMMIGRANTS IN THE UNITED STATES OF AMERICA, HIDDEN PEOPLE FROM ALL OVER THE WORLD MAY BE PRESENT. ELEMENTALS OF THE PRIMORDIAL CREATURE CLASS ARE ENTIRELY A'NOWALKÓWAN, THOUGH THEY MAY BE CALLED BY THEIR MOST RECOGNIZABLE COMMON-USE NAME.

HIDDEN PEOPLE

As this is a training primer and as this particular class of Elemental beings is so broad, we will only offer a very brief overview here. For more granular study of specific Hidden Peoples, please consult with the Order of St. Catherine and Her Archives.

Hidden People have interacted with humans the world over from time immemorial. They are elemental beings whose power and peculiarities vary by region, culture, and time, but they tend to exhibit certain unifying traits: they are not always visible to the human eye and may go unseen if they wish; they have supernatural powers beyond any which humans are capable of wielding, many of which they may use reflexively and without ritual; they may be appeased by offerings and often exhibit a preference for sweets;

they have instinctive attraction or aversion to certain substances, symbols, or sounds. They are usually associated with elements or natural features, including deep water, dry and arid landscapes, caves, and frozen wastes, though there is a subclass that has taken a liking to human homes. In many traditions, they live in naturally-occurring rings of stones or flora, or under hills and mounds. While they can make themselves invisible, they may also choose to take an animal or human form to covertly observe humans. However, even when they appear human, they usually exhibit unnatural features that hint at their supernatural character. They are often mischievous, but not always. While they are called many names, the most recognizable categories to the layperson would be fairies, jinn, kami, or any number of variations of "little people" or "good neighbors."

Hidden Folk magic is often difficult to undo—if it can be undone at all by human means. It exhibits traits of what is traditionally considered first-degree magic, such as total transfiguration of themselves or objects or conjuring objects from seemingly nothing. There is some debate, however, over whether this is truly first-degree magic or simply a "sleight-of-hand" accomplished by manipulating the boundary between our world and theirs. Some of their magical capabilities are indisputably limited expressions of first-degree magic, and thus they command—indeed, demand—a high degree of respect and wariness from Knights.

We have included below some broad characterization of certain Hidden Folk. This is for basic informative purposes and not intended to be deeply descriptive or prescriptive, nor is it comprehensive or all-inclusive. The Hidden People named below are a cross-section of possible Hidden People a knight might encounter, not a complete list.

Generally, FAIRIES are a class of being that populates the northern and western parts of Europe; they are often associated in one way or another with bodies of water, though of course there are significant exceptions. They are, to a one, clever, mischievous, and intensely proud beings. They place a high value on words, particularly names, and also proper conduct in their company. One might say they value "honor" as well, but it is a kind of honor that is at turns alien to our own and thus cannot be relied upon when interacting with them. Some fairies are mostly harmless, capable of performing malicious little tricks or pranks and little more—often, the subjects of these minor jinxes have, indeed, done something untoward and must simply accept their just desserts. Others pose a much more significant danger to mankind, such as The Wild Hunt and Undines (nixies, naiads, sirens and their like). Some few are quite affable and seem to enjoy helping humans, provided they are treated well. IN ALL CIRCUMSTANCES, the most important fact for a knight to recall is to NEVER "GIVE" A FAIRY ONE'S TRUE NAME. There are several ways to circumlocute this trap whenever it arises, such as offering a temporary use-name, but such is a topic covered in greater depth in more advanced training materials.

The best defense against fairies is avoiding their notice or places frequented by them; however, when duty calls, a knight must respond. Fairies may be repelled or, in extreme cases, banished or killed by use of cold iron. Rowan may also be used to protect against fairies, though this seems a less universal and less effective means than cold iron. The Order, however, strongly urges against use of lethal force in the case of fairies, even in extreme cases. The reasons for this are myriad. In brief, not only are they sapient beings whose right to life must fundamentally be respected, but they are also Elementals, which means they are intimately connected to the proper functioning of the natural world around us. The death of one at the hands of a knight might also cause a serious conflict between fairies and humans (see the Bourscheid Debacle of 1441 and the Foz Incident of 1512) that may only be assuaged at great cost.

The JINN are the hidden people of Northern Africa, the Levant and Near East, and certain sections of Central Europe and Asia, though their range is broad and may expand beyond even these. They are often associated with air and fire and with abandoned or desolate places, though they may be connected to any number of elements or landscape features. They are incredibly varied in temperament, function, and form. Some of their number possess a staggering control of first-degree magic, though it seems they are incapable of leveraging it without explicit direction. There are many theories as to why this might be the case, but as this is not salient to the training materials here, we will leave it to the reader to investigate further at their leisure.

Jinn, even moreso than fairies, often live lives parallel to our own. A good portion of them spend their days just as we do, merely a breath's-span away on the other side of the Veil which separates our world from theirs. They are largely social, though there are a number of solitary Jinn that seem to shun the company of man and other Jinn alike. Many Jinn are curious about humans and pass among us in animal or human forms, though in human form they usually have some imperfection which indicates their preternatural nature, such as backward-facing feet[1].

Various talismans and charms have been used since Antiquity to repel Jinn or invoke their powers of protection. Jinn may choose to work in partnership with humans and human lineages of their own free will. Others may exercise their abilities on behalf of a human on a temporary basis, usually to discharge a debt they feel they have incurred. But some practitioners have developed techniques for capturing Jinn and commanding them—this is perhaps when Jinn pose the greatest threat to knights.

When harmed or slighted, Jinn may temporarily possess an offending human or curse them with foul luck. Both usually run their course and are best left to more specialized communities to handle, but occasionally circumstances demand that the Order intervene. Typically Jinn acknowledge and respond to the power

---

[1] However, NO KNIGHT SHOULD ASSUME BASED ON DEFORMITY OR DISABILITY ALONE THAT A PERSON IS A JINN. Knights must conduct themselves in a considerate, temperate, methodical way; it is uncouth in the extreme to hurl accusations at any-body, let alone a crippled or disfigured person attempting to live their life in public.

of Allah or any other name of the monotheistic Abrahamic God, but this is not always the case. Like many Hidden People, Jinn have a deep aversion to iron, which may be used as ward or weapon against them. Much like with fairies, it is strongly advised not to use violence against Jinn, as this is both improper and risks triggering a larger conflict with the Jinn tribes.

NVNEHI are a friendly Hidden People native to the Appalachian Mountains of North America. They enjoy a particularly close relationship with the Cherokee people, though they have appeared in recent years to settlers of foreign descent as well, usually communities of people who have lived peacefully and respectfully in the mountains alongside the Cherokee for multiple generations. Usually they are invisible, their presence detected only by overhearing their singing and drumming. When they do choose to reveal themselves, they most often appear as Cherokee people, though some reports claim they may choose to match the ethnicity of anyone they approach. Like many Hidden People, they enjoy music, particularly singing and dancing, and are attracted to celebrations and particularly gifted individuals who might be singing or practicing their instrument in solitude. Nvnehi are known to help people in need, sometimes by guiding or sheltering them in foul weather conditions, sometimes by warning them of disasters, and occasionally by fighting on behalf of defenseless people. While Nvnehi are overwhelmingly peace-loving and do not seem to pose any significant risk to knights or laypeople, it is advised that should a knight be invited to stay in the Nvnehi Otherland for a time (perhaps to wait out a storm or hide from a larger threat), she must not eat the food of the

Nvnehi. Like with most food in Adjacencies, once consumed, it makes it difficult or impossible to leave the Adjacency[2]. Likewise, time moves differently in Adjacencies; knights must take care to leave them as soon as possible, for the duration of her stay may prove to be far longer than she might suspect.

To date, Order interactions with Nvnehi have been nothing but cordial, and Nvnehi act with force only in defense of otherwise defenseless people. Of the Hidden Peoples, they are fairly straightforward in their dealings with humans, and they can be trusted to act forthrightly. Knights are commanded to act with the utmost care, respect, and good faith toward Nvnehi.

AZIZA are a Little People most often reported in the American East. Like Jinn and Fairies they are a transplant to these shores, having followed West African colonists from the Beninese Empire to A'nowalkówa. Most reports agree that they are a small people about the size of an ant; consequently, they live in dwellings that resemble anthills or sometimes make their homes in certain trees, particularly silk-cotton trees. They live exclusively in forests and grant good luck to people who show the proper respect toward their environment and demonstrate thoughtful hunting practices.

---

[2] For this reason among many others, every knight venturing forth into a wilderness area is required to pack emergency food rations in her kit. If she runs out while Away, she should begin taking the iron pills packed in her emergency rations with every Adjacency meal. This protocol has shown promise in slowing the preternaturalization and other supernatural effects of Adjacency foods.

Such worthy individuals may be the beneficiaries of aid from Aziza in the event any misfortune befalls them, or they may be granted visions and supernatural knowledge that the Aziza deem equal to their valor.

Aziza seem to keep mostly to themselves, though if they see behavior in their woods they feel impertinent, they may play harmless but unnerving tricks on trespassers. Still, they are not a militant group, and the Order has no history of dispute with them. Order knights should take care to be mindful about their conduct whilst moving through forests—a commendable practice regardless of preternatural pressures.

DEMI-DEMONIC HUMANS

Though their incidence is so rare as to be nearly negligible, their existence and properties are such as to be worth mentioning.

In truth, not much is understood about demi-demonic humans precisely because of their vanishingly small numbers. Within the entirety of Order records, knights have encountered demi-demons six times. Prior to the Order's founding, evidence from legends and folklore around the globe hint at perhaps nine more, though there is no indication any of these older ones are still extant. It is thought that demi-demons are what happens when a demon possessing a human somehow becomes entangled with the human soul, ultimately reaching a balance and sharing the body with its host without subjugating their mind or spirit. Two of the demi-demons recorded in the Order Archives seem to have been the result of spontaneous possessions that, by mechanisms unknown, resulted in this symbiosis. The other four were sorcerers who, through conjuration and ritual, invited the demons into themselves and transformed. Of note is the fact that these were the only four that survived this process; evidence through the ages suggests that others have tried only to suffer gruesome deaths instead. It is unknown why some individuals survive the process while others do not.

Upon transformation, the demi-demon gains a number of supernatural characteristics: luminous eyes, often of a disturbing hue; remarkable strength, such that surpasses even a vampire's; unusual speed, slightly less as seen in a vampire; ungodly constitution and a unique ability to heal nearly instantaneously from fatal blows; and the ability to perceive magic as plainly as an average human might any other primary sense.

These by themselves are a frightening combination, but more novel and disturbing still is their innate ability to warp the magic in their immediate vicinity, and, when the demon is ascendant, the emergence of a supernatural aura which strikes terror and agony into the souls of any human near to it.

While not necessarily immortal, it is believed that demi-demons age slowly, perhaps allowing them to survive hundreds of years. The oldest demi-demon encountered by Order knights was purportedly approaching four hundred years old and appeared to be no more than forty before her execution, necessitated when she massacred two entire villages in the Swiss Alps in 1643.

Due to their preternaturally robust constitution, the only known way of slaying a demi-demon is by complete decapitation. Because of their strength and speed, it is advised that no less than three knights be tasked with dispatching one, with five to seven being ideal.

ALSO BY J. M. LINKHART

First-Degree Magic

MORE FROM THE JOANIVERSE:

The Harrowing of Minerva Damson (podcast)
The Delilah Documents (podcast, Patreon exclusive)

ABOUT THE AUTHOR

J. M. Linkhart lives in Oklahoma with her husband and friends. Together, they do silly little things like produce podcasts and make their own costumes for renaissance fairs. Like most authors she is a book hoarder, and she has a special love for history and cookbooks (and anything that combines the two). A social media cryptid, she generally avoids being seen but will occasionally pop up to remind people that yes, she does exist actually. You might catch a glimpse of her on any of Goblin Booth Productions' social media platforms (listed below) or perhaps at a book signing somewhere. You can certainly hear her on any of the podcasts currently produced by Goblin Booth Productions, if podcasts are your thing.

Instagram: @goblinboothproductions and @jmlinkharttheauthor
Patreon: www.patreon.com/theharrowingofminervadamson
YouTube: www.youtube.com/goblinboothproductions

Check out our podcasts on our website at goblinboothproductions. com, or search for them on any major podcasting platform:

The Harrowing of Minerva Damson

Route 6.6

This Book SUCKS!

Media Morsels